ROBERT'S HILL

(or the time I pooped my snowsuit)

AND OTHER CHRISTMAS STORIES

Robert's HILL

(or the time I pooped my snowsuit) AND OTHER CHRISTMAS STORIES

JEREMY JOHN

DUNDURN
PRESS

Publisher: Scott Fraser | Acquiring editor: Kathryn Lane | Editor: Melissa Kawaguchi
Cover designer: Laura Boyle
Cover image: Sledder: shutterstock.com/By nik_orl; scrollwork: istock.com/mxtama
Interior images: pikisuperstar/Freepik

Library and Archives Canada Cataloguing in Publication

Title: Robert's Hill, or, The time I pooped my snowsuit : and other Christmas stories
    / Jeremy John.
Other titles: Time I pooped my snowsuit.
Names: John, Jeremy, author.
Description: Short stories.
Identifiers: Canadiana (print) 20210324414 | Canadiana (ebook) 20210277998 | ISBN
    9781459750166 (softcover) | ISBN 9781459749399 (PDF) | ISBN 9781459749405
    (EPUB)
Classification: LCC PS8619.O4445 R63 2021 | DDC C813/.6—dc23

We acknowledge the support of the Canada Council for the Arts and the Ontario Arts Council for our publishing program. We also acknowledge the financial support of the Government of Ontario, through the Ontario Book Publishing Tax Credit and Ontario Creates, and the Government of Canada.

Printed and bound in Canada.

Dundurn Press
1382 Queen Street East
Toronto, Ontario, Canada M4L 1C9
dundurn.com, @dundurnpress 🐦 f 📷

This book is dedicated to family. Mine and yours.
Mine is a wonderfully odd group of characters; many share
the same ancestry, and many do not.
But they are my family.
Whomever your family includes, however you celebrate each
other, these stories are for you.

Contents

Introduction

THIS COLLECTION IS a long-running tradition in my family. It started a few decades ago, when I was very young and asked my father what he wanted for Christmas. He asked me to write him a story. I guess he was all stocked up on ties and socks.

Every year since then, we have gathered together for a new story. Sometimes we were sitting on big couches beside the tree. Sometimes we were at the table, still working on our second pieces of pumpkin pie. Sometimes we travelled very far distances to be together. Sometimes we gathered together online because we were just too far away. Sometimes guests, who would eventually become family, would wonder at our odd tradition.

Sometimes the stories were written specifically for the kids, because they think pooping your snowsuit is funny. Sometimes the stories were written for the grown-ups, because they think pooping your snowsuit is funny. Other times I was looking to answer questions. Like, what is the best Christmas movie ("The Greatest Christmas Movie of All Time Ever"), or how was the candy cane invented ("The Sweet Things")? Some were written for specific people, like my second child, whose birthday is December 25th ("Never Open a Present on Christmas Eve: A Cautionary Tale"), or inspired by an urban legend ("The Twelve Shots of Christmas"). Some are very new ("The Christmas Divorce"), while others were written a long time ago ("Merry Christmas, Mr. Baggins").

Some stories were very good and became favourites of my friends and family. Others were not included in this collection. But the one thing that never changed was that when I read these stories, we were together. That was the whole point. These are stories about family, for family. For a little while each year, I am able to bring my family together and share something that says, "I've missed seeing you," "I'm glad we are all here together," and "I love you."

I hope that this book does the same for you. I hope it brings you together with your family and gives you a chance to say "Merry Christmas."

Robert's Hill
(or The Time I Pooped My Snowsuit)

IT WAS CHRISTMAS 1982, and I was the fat kid. No surprise.
I had been the fat kid for the ten Christmases before that,
so this was nothing special. But this time I was the fat kid
with the hottest toy of the season. At least that is what the
commercials said. But most important was the fact that I had
one and none of my friends did. Not that I had many friends.
I was the fat kid, after all. But none of them had what I had.

I raced to the phone, as all the other presents had been
opened, and made four quick calls.

Andy, Darren, Jeff Marcella, and that smelly kid whose
name I can't remember anymore. It's funny looking back
— for the life of me, I can't remember his name. But even
now, after all these years, whenever someone burns a grilled
cheese sandwich, I think of him.

I called my four best, and only, friends in order of their popularity. Darren, then Jeff Marcella, then stinky kid, and then Andy. Andy may not have been fat, but he certainly wasn't very popular.

The conversation was the same with each of my friends that morning. When they answered the phone, I quickly asked them what they got first so I could save the best — my present, the hottest toy of the season — for last. They finished their lists with something like, "Ah and my mom got me some clothes and junk." And I'd say something nice, like, "Oh that's great" — then a dramatic pause and BAM — "Guess what, I got a GT Snowracer!"

Just like that, with a few simple words, I went from being the fat kid … to being the fat kid with a cool new toy. It may not seem like much, but in the fickle world of grade-school friends, it moved me all the way up to Darren's level of popularity. Which was a big jump from my usual tie with the kid who smelled like charred cheese.

According to the commercial, the GT Snowracer was the ultimate in downhill sledding technology. The ads had scenes of teenagers ankle deep in clean white snow, smiling from ear to ear, as a huge group of friends joined in the fun and their parents looked on proudly.

This was not an ancient toboggan built from heavy slats of wood. No, my friends. The all-black beauty had a "powder-coated tubular frame created using high impact plastic that took thirty years to develop." My god, it even came from Sweden. From the first time I saw that commercial to each of the three thousand times I saw it again before that day, I was looking forward to the time when I

4

would "enjoy the thrill and excitement of sledding in a way you have never experienced before."

No one was able to leave the house that day. So, the first run would have to wait until Boxing Day. Which meant I had twenty-four hours to prepare. The trick was to make sure that all the most popular kids walked away saying, "Wasn't that GT Snowracer that Jeremy had just great?" and *not*, "wasn't that GT Snowracer that the fat kid had just great?" This was certainly tricky, but I had a lot of time to plan out the perfect afternoon.

I decided I would arrive early. Get in a few trial runs. Just to make sure I knew what I was doing and that I looked good when my friends arrived. The guys would start showing up, and they'd ask about the GT. I would rave about my new gift, but not too much. You don't want to oversell it. Then they'd ask for a turn.

I'd explain that I still wanted to get in one more run, to check the steering or maybe try a different path down the hill. You know, letting the anticipation build.

Then I would slowly hand it over, so that they knew it was precious. Then I'd offer some final words of wisdom, something to remind them that I was an expert in the subtleties of controlling this finely crafted plastic Swedish speed machine.

I'd say something like, "If it gets too fast, you're going to want to bail out. That's only natural. But remember the handbrake, and if anything goes wrong, try to steer toward open snow." I'd reassure them with a pat on the shoulder and watch them cruise down the hill smiling. After they stopped at the bottom, I would shout out something like,

"That was pretty good, for your first time." They would trudge up the hill as fast as they could. Not only to beg me for another turn but also to congratulate me on my gift, compliment me on my bravery, and marvel at my generosity.

It was the perfect plan, and there was no way anything could possibly go wrong.

December 26. Darren, Jeff Marcella, Andy, and the kid who smelled like barbecued parmesan would be at Robert's Hill by noon. I had to beat them there. Nothing could stop me from leaving on time. Except for food.

Mom had just taken lunch out of the oven, so I put my sledding plans on hold to grab a bite. I was the fat kid, after all, and you don't become the fat kid by choosing to go outside and play when there is a meal waiting. Plus, it was my favourite, shepherd's pie, and I was only going to have one piece.

After my second piece, I grabbed four cookies. Just in case I got hungry on the way there. Because, as the fat kid, I had noticed that I got hungry a lot more often than other people. Then, just a little behind schedule, I was out the door.

I walked the five minutes to Robert's Hill, and already things didn't look good. I was sweaty, and I had eaten all my cookies. Worse, there were tons of kids on the hill. Even worse, they were big kids, and they all had GT Snowracers. Plus, all my friends were already at the top of the hill waiting. The only good news was that there was no way the big kids would share, so mine would still be the first GT that my friends would go on.

I trudged up the hill as my four friends yelled at me to hurry up. When I got to the top I was badly out of breath. It was a very big hill. Then again, to the fat kid, every hill is a very big hill. Darren didn't even say hi. He just asked me if he could go first. I meant to say something that made me sound like I had his best interest at heart, but, exhausted, I just mumbled, "No ... me ... expert ... check brakes ... so it is safe." I turned and faced the south side of the hill, then smiled at the calming scene before me. I looked out at clean white snow as it gradually dropped away from the summit and opened out onto a large field. That pristine landscape told me one important thing: My perfect plan could be saved with one good run.

I stepped toward the south side with new-found confidence, then one of the older kids said, "Hey, look he's going on the baby hill." One of the other teenagers looked at me and said, "Hey, fat kid, why don't you try this side. If you wipe out, try to land on your belly." But that side was never meant for tobogganing. It was essentially a forest with a one-hundred-foot vertical drop. That side of Robert's Hill was hard enough to walk down during the summer. Covered in snow, it was impossible for any child on any toboggan to go down that side of the hill and survive.

Ah, but a small gang of neighbourhood teenagers, with a little help from the Swedish designers at GT, had changed all that. Not only had these daredevils opened up the north face of Robert's Hill, but their suicidal runs had packed down the snow between the trees. It was now as slick as a bobsled run. I could see from the summit that one of the trees had crash marks on it, with shards of broken sled scattered at the base of the trunk. About halfway down, a thorny bush held someone's toque high in the air as a warning to any other unskilled sled pilot.

I was sure that if the trees did not kill me, the bushes would. However, I had no choice but to go down the north run. Plus, I had to make it look good. I was in front of not only my friends but also the big kids, who had stopped to watch, as well. On the upside, if I could somehow pull this off, I would increase my status at my school, and I could theoretically begin building a reputation at the high school. With a stellar run, maybe when I walked into high school people would look at me and say, "Hey, that's the kid who made that killer GT run on Robert's Hill. I hear he used to be fat."

I lined up my GT for the inside of turn one and pushed off as gently as I could. In just the first two feet of sliding, my Swedish-made, three-skied, powder-coated tubular-frame speed machine accelerated like it was an F1 race car. The first hairpin turn was upon me before I even had a chance to reach for the brake. I turned the world's first mass-produced steerable sled all the way to the right and skidded across the slick packed snow, curling around the outer limbs of a pine tree on my starboard side. I had a moment to take a deep breath, and then turn two was in front of me. It was a bend of slightly less than ninety degrees with a thorny bush on the uphill side, waiting to tear my face and skewer my eyeballs if I failed to make the turn. On the downhill side was the trunk of an oak tree that was four feet wide and had probably been breaking bones of tobogganers since the sled was first invented. Like a chubby toque-wearing captain of a catamaran, I leaned as far to the left as I could, pushing the downhill ski into the snow, trying to make the turn. When I finally rounded the corner, the pom-pom on my toque had brushed the skull crusher on my left, and the right sleeve of my hand-me-down coat had been grazed by a dozen razor-sharp thorns. Coming out of the corner I straightened out the sled and began silently cursing the people of Sweden and everything that had ever come out of that godforsaken country. That's when I really started picking up speed. I was now moving so fast that the wind burned my cheeks and partially frozen tears blurred my vision. I was barely able to see what was ahead, let alone avoid it. The big kids had constructed a ramp at the end of the line of trees. It must have been twenty feet tall and probably took a team of engineers four weeks to complete.

I was airborne before I even had time to panic, which was good because if I had had more time, I would have seriously freaked out. But if by some fluke of luck I was able to survive the landing, I would easily become a legend among my group of friends. And in a few months, when I was released from the hospital, they would all come to see my cool scars and the machine that would help me breathe. If I survived, I could become very popular.

I stood on the two side skis, leaning out over the steering wheel like an Olympic ski jumper in an effort to balance myself as I soared off the mammoth jump. My only hope was to put my faith in a bunch of nerdy toboggan designers in Sweden. I held on to the belief that the front shock absorbers and the steel handbrake would be my saviours. The shock absorbers did nothing, and the handbrake just made things worse.

Now, normally in the human body, the digestive system works very slowly. To pass through the six metres of the small intestine, it usually takes food up to eight hours to complete the trip. Then the one-and-a-half-metre trip through the large intestine takes another twenty-four hours. Apparently, this does not apply to shepherd's pie. What resulted was due to a dangerous combination of grease-covered beef and the tooth-loosening impact of a fall from twenty-five feet. Something, probably shepherd's pie, somewhere, probably in my colon, was knocked loose, and I pooped my snowsuit.

In a complete panic, I stood up. Bad idea. The upward momentum and the effect of gravity began to threaten the cleanliness of my snow boots. So, I sat back down. Bad idea. The earlier meal was now making its way above my belt and into my coat. I compromised with a half squat that would both keep the mess where it was and allow me to apply the steel handbrake. The left side broke as soon as it touched the snow. But in my panic, I was pulling so hard that the right side dug in deep and turned the sled ninety degrees to the right in the blink of an eye. I was thrown downhill, spinning in the air as I flew. I saw a muted-yellow winter sun and a clear-blue sky just before my skull hit the ground.

My mouth slammed shut and my chin hit my chest as I landed back on the ground. A simple combination of downward momentum and having my neck exposed allowed the back of my winter coat to fill with snow and small frozen rocks. I skidded to a halt on my back as my beloved ultra-light luge slowly slid down the hill past me.

There was nothing I could do. I stood up and walked to my GT. Giving my friends a clear view of my back was a considerable risk. But I believed that the two inches of snow that covered me from head to toe would hide anything that had had a chance to leak through. Without even breaking stride, I grabbed the seat of the Snowracer and tucked it under my arm.

There was nothing else to do. No way to explain. No way to cover it up. I simply started for home.

After about ten steps I started to think that maybe my friends hadn't noticed. Maybe they weren't watching. Maybe I was too far away to be seen. Then Darren yelled out, "Where are you going?"

Without turning around, I yelled, "I'm going home."

I got home, cleaned up, ate a bag of chips, and asked my mom if I could transfer to another school.

The Twelve Shots of Christmas

SOME CHRISTMAS TRADITIONS should never be repeated, and my whole family is grateful that this never happened again. It was about a week before Christmas and for the first time, everyone in the house was of drinking age. My older brother, Paul, was back from university for his Christmas break, and Dad asked, "Who wants a drink?" I had been of drinking age for about three months now, and that was more than enough time to figure out that I wasn't much of a drinker. It made me sleepy at best and sick at worst. I never did understand the appeal, but that wasn't the case for my dad and my brother. Dad liked Scotch, and my brother liked beer, and both already had one going when Mom said, "I'll have a small glass of wine." Dad opened a beer for me before I could say no, so it looked like I was having one, too.

Dad sat down in his recliner with a loud exhale and said what I remember him saying every time he ever touched the TV remote: "Let's see what's on the old boob tube." And then he started flicking through channels. This was obviously from the pre-colonial times, before every show was on-demand and channels were searchable. Back then you had to watch whatever was on TV at that moment.

Dad started at the first channel and was in the upper teens when Mom chipped in, "You need to slow down. You change the channels too fast. How can you even see what's on?" Dad took a sip and looked over the top of the glass at me, never breaking eye contact while he played with Mom. Now, he was flipping the channels slowly, really slowly, then clicked past ten stations in a row without a pause, then he went back one, then forward one, then back one, then forward one, then back one. He kept this up until Mom said, "Fine, pick whatever you want." Then Dad burst out laughing, banging his glass down on the coffee table. Now that I think about it, Dad may have had more than just one drink at this point.

Dad kept flipping for something to watch, and then Mom got serious. She gave Dad a sly smile, reached out, and said, "Give me the remote and I'll pick something." It was a classic living-room play for dominance. Dad had seen this before, and he wasn't about to let Mom get her hands on his authority.

"Okay," he said, moving the remote to the hand farthest from my mother, "what do you want to watch?"

"It's Christmas time, so see if you can find a Christmas movie." Mom had proven her point and sat back with her glass of wine. "Something classic, like *Home Alone*, or something uplifting, like *The Polar Express*, or something fun, like *The Muppet Christmas Carol*."

Dad started flipping, and my brother groaned. "All those movies are terrible."

"You don't like *The Muppet Christmas Carol*?" My mom said it like she was genuinely offended, as if she had written the script instead of just having rented the movie once in 1988.

Paul was in his second year of university and had taken an elective in film studies; therefore, he was an absolute expert in every film ever made. Although, it seemed like the only thing he learned was that any popular movie was terrible, and all the best movies were ones that you had never heard of. "The biggest problem with *The Muppet Christmas Carol* is that it fails to deliver on either promised front. It is neither a strong telling of the classic Dickens story, nor is it engaging enough to be a stand-alone Muppet movie. See, this one was the first Muppet project after the passing of Jim Henson, so it's missing its traditional Muppet heart and soul. Instead, this one was directed by Frank Oz, which probably goes a long way to explain Michael Caine's poor performance. He acts like he's reading his lines off a cue card that he's never seen before. That movie has got to be the only example of an Oscar winner being out-acted by the guy who had his hand shoved up Miss Piggy's butt."

You know what, maybe my brother had had a few drinks before I got there, too.

While I couldn't tell you what the girls in university thought about my brother's new-found knowledge, I knew that my mom was less than impressed. "So, Mr. Movie Expert, how about *Home Alone*? Can we watch that instead?"

Dad got up and headed to the bar in the corner of the room. "Don't encourage him, Cynth," he said. Mom's name was Cynthia, but I don't remember Dad ever calling her that. It was always Cynth.

"Come on now, what could be wrong with little Kevin McCallister learning that deep down his family really loves him?"

Paul put his left elbow down on the back of the couch and tilted his beer bottle toward our mom, accepting the challenge. "That movie isn't about a loving family. It's about a terrible family. Mr. and Mrs. McCallister are bad parents, and not just for forgetting Kevin at home."

Mom leaned back on her elbow, realizing that she had made a mistake, a long-winded and boring mistake.

"The McCallisters are terrible parents for the way they treat Kevin," Paul said. He took a sip of his drink to add a dramatic pause. "For the entire opening act, he is ignored. They barely acknowledge that he's part of the family until the Pepsi gets spilled in the pizza. Then they let Uncle Frank call him names. In front of the whole family he says, 'Look at what you did, you little jerk.' What kind of person says that to their eight-year-old nephew? What kind of parent lets a grown-up speak to their child that way? Mom, you wouldn't let your brother talk to us like that. Dad, you wouldn't let Uncle Mike talk to us like that."

Dad was back from pouring himself a double, or it might have been a triple, and he lowered himself back into the La-Z-Boy. "You're damn right, son. I'd knock his lights out. Hey, that sounds like fun. Let's get him over here instead of watching a movie." He started to laugh. "Cynth, call your brother up and invite him to meet us behind the woodshed."

Mom slapped at Dad. She couldn't reach him from her spot on the couch; it was more just a way to tell him to shush. "Right, sorry," said Dad, taking a sip and talking under his breath, just loud enough so everyone could hear. "Right, you're right. After all, no one knows where he is right now." Paused, then took a sip. "We know where he isn't ... at work." Dad chuckled to himself and went back to flipping channels in search of the perfect Christmas movie.

Paul continued unprompted, "And *The Polar Express* is less of a movie and more of a CGI experiment. They just threw in Tom Hanks, hoping that audiences would be distracted by the most overused actor in Hollywood." Paul felt he was on a roll and wasn't about to stop now. "You see, the overly sentimental story is made even more saccharine so the audience will overlook Robert Zemeckis playing around with a performance-capture technology, even though Peter Jackson had already shown the world how to do it right in 2001."

I could tell Mom wanted to move to the end of the conversation a little faster. She said, "So, what is the best Christmas movie, then?"

Paul gave his I-was-hoping-you-would-ask smile and brushed back his hair. "There is a small black-and-white French film, really an homage to the early work of director Jean-Luc Colliar ..."

Dad was done with this conversation and was going to end it now, politely or not. "How about this one?" Dad stopped flipping. "Is there anything wrong with this one?" he said as he took a sip. "And if there is, keep it to yourself."

"Nah, Dad, this one's fine," Paul said, sitting back and smiling at the old man.

"Oh, I like this one, George. Nice pick." Mom got up and walked up beside Dad's armchair. "You boys look hungry. I'll make you a snack." According to Mom, we always looked hungry. Thank goodness we inherited a fast metabolism. Of course, that wouldn't last forever.

As the opening credits began, so did Paul. He had changed his tone, but continued to show off. "The movie is really a series of loosely tied together short stories. The originals were written by a guy named Jean Sheppard, and some of the stuff was actually written as short stories for *Playboy* magazine." I remember Dad laughing at this fact. "No, it's true, Dad. The other parts of the movie are stories that Sheppard told on the radio and on the college lecture circuit." He had Dad's genuine attention and wasn't going to give it up now.

For us boys, getting Dad to pay attention was always tough if it didn't involve sports. Having Dad focus on you, without having to risk your life on the football field, was always a special accomplishment. "If I remember correctly" — and of course you know he did — "the story that got the director Bob Clark interested in making the movie was called 'Flick's Tongue,' you know, where the kid gets dared to put his tongue on the metal pole."

Dad looked back at my brother and me on the couch and smiled as he said, "I triple-dog dare you."

Paul laughed and pressed his advantage. "Actually, TBS holds a movie marathon every year, and they show it twelve times in a row. The whole thing lasts almost exactly twenty-four hours." Really, he was just being a jerk now. That last part wasn't necessary at all.

At that point, Mom walked in with a tray of food and we all sat down to watch *A Christmas Story*.

Now, pause.

You could say it was my fault.

When my brother tells this story, he usually opens with that. "It was all his fault. I just wanted to watch a movie." Maybe he was right, but like all the biggest mistakes in life, it takes more than just one person. I think the fault deserves to be equally shared by everyone, except Mom. Mom was an innocent bystander. Then again, she never did anything to stop us.

Right, Mom was guilty, too.

Maybe it was because Paul was getting all the attention. I'm not really sure why I said it, but he was right — I was the one who mentioned it. "You know, there's actually a drinking game based on this movie." Dad seemed interested, and now it was my turn for Dad's attention. "Yeah, super simple, you just have a drink every time someone says 'Ralphie.'"

Dad chuckled, and the movie started. I hadn't been able to wow him with facts about the author and the director, but at least I had gotten my small share of Dad's attention. The movie started with the iconic voice-over:

Ah, there it is. My house.

And good old Cleveland Street. How could I ever forget it?

And there I am, with that dumb round face and ...

that stupid stocking cap.

But no matter. Christmas was on its way.

It's only seconds later that the little boy has his attention ripped away from the store window containing the Red Ryder BB gun, when his mother calls his name, Ralphie. With that, my brother finished his beer, leaned over to my Dad's side of the coffee table, and plunked down the empty. "Come on, Dad, finish up. She said 'Ralphie.'" Dad's head turned on a swivel; he knew when he was being challenged. Like an aging lion facing a challenge for the head of the pride, he had no choice but to put on a show of strength. His Jack and Coke was still mostly full, but he downed it anyway. Then he turned to collect my brother's empty and carried his own glass to the bar. I was the one who said, "Come on, Mom, you're in this, too." But she was having none of that. She took a small sip and said to me, "Oh no, don't forget. We are all going to church tomorrow morning."

Funny that none of us questioned her about that. She was the only one who went to church regularly. Dad only went when Mom made him. Paul and I only went at Christmas, and only because she insisted. All these years later I kind of miss it. No, actually, I don't miss church. I miss Mom. And all of my strongest memories of her happened in that place. I can remember her doing lots of other things with us, but the memories of her sitting beside Dad in the pew are so much more vivid. I can see thin blurry pictures of her in my head from when she took us to football practice or when she was working in her garden. But when I remember her at church on Christmas Eve, I can hear the songs, I can smell the incense, I can see the green coat she was wearing. The pictures are so vivid and complete it feels like I could move around the room in my memory. I see each line on her face as she's singing. I remember her smile as she chatted with the priest on the way out of mass.

As you might expect, we never made it to mass the next morning.

Before Ralphie was finished with his daydream about saving his family with his BB gun, or, as I'm sure Mr. Know-It-All would have said, "A Red Ryder, Carbine Action, 200-shot Range Model air rifle, with a compass in the stock and this thing that tells time," my dad was back from the bar. And he was about to escalate the evening. He set down a tray with four shot glasses filled with Jack Daniel's. "If you boys are going to do this, we're going to do this right." But he didn't just say "boys," he said "BOOOYS," a verbal dropping of the gauntlet. With a couple extra syllables, he had taken off his white glove and slapped us both across the face.

My brother, maybe trying to back down gracefully, maybe trying to save us all, for whatever reason, tried to decline. "Woah, Dad. I don't think you know how many times they say his name in this movie. He is the main character, after all."

Almost on cue, like this television was waiting for that exact moment, Melinda Dillon, the actress who would later in the movie accidentally break the famous leg lamp, looked out into our living room and uttered those two dangerous syllables, "Ralphie." Not missing a moment, Dad picked up the nearest shot glass. He looked back at my brother and me, smiled, and said, "I triple-dog dare you."

We all drank.

That was number one.

Numbers two and three came at the start of the scene where the old man is fighting with the furnace and the little brother can't put his arm down because of his snowsuit. Not too bad. One shot at the beginning of the scene and one at the end, spaced out nicely. Dad had time to get from the La-Z-Boy to the bar and back again before he needed to pour out the second round.

It was around this time that Mom went upstairs to bed. She was good with stuff like this. I mean knowing when it was a time for boys to be with their fathers. I bet not having any daughters was hard on her, but she seemed to instinctively know when a son needed his dad and when a boy needed his mom.

The scene where Flick is dared to stick his tongue to the frozen pole is a classic, and in fact, the name *Ralphie* is not said once during the sequence. I can't think of a time I've heard my dad laugh as hard as he did that night. He actually clapped when Schwartz said that line "I triple-dog dare you," and threw himself back into his recliner laughing when Miss Shields goes to the window to see Flick alone in the desolate schoolyard, crying with his tongue stuck to a pole.

There is one more shot when Ralphie gets home from school, then another in his dream about his school assignment, yet another one when Ralphie rescues Flash Gordon. The shots were coming fast and furious now. Dad had given up on the mad dash to the bar and had brought the bottle to the table somewhere in between shots three and four. At this point Dad and Paul were still going toe to toe, both downing their shots without even a grimace. Dad had about twenty years of training under his belt. With his poker nights, weekends at the cottage, and his famous summer barbecues, this was not a new experience for Dad. What my older brother lacked in experience he more than made up for with his youth. At twenty-one years old, his body could handle any bad decision he made. I, however, had neither quality. I was already in over my head, and we were just at the first commercial break. We all dug into the snacks, everyone opting for chips or crackers to help absorb the booze.

When the commercial was done, Dad poured a round of shots and the movie opened with the leg-lamp scene. The dad is wonderful in that scene, standing across the road to see what the lamp looks like, basking in the glow of electric sex. We all laughed at this part, maybe it was the shots, but we shouldn't have been laughing. That scene is a set-up. It is designed to relax you and get you to drop your guard. Casual drinkers, be warned, because the next part is going to finish you off. The first few "Ralphies" are just left-handed jabs, setting you up for a big right hook. The scene in the bathroom is the knockout punch and you never see it coming.

Ralphie heads upstairs to listen to the *Little Orphan Annie* radio show, locks the bathroom door, and pulls out his decoder ring — and that's when the trouble starts. Little brother Randy is outside and wants in, so what does he do? He says "Ralphie" over and over and over again. Dad was pouring shots and handing them out as fast as he could. Mumbling out a "there's another one," or a "one more for you," or the occasional "holy crap" as he picked up the bottle again and again. My brother was helping out and laughing the whole time. "There's another one, Dad," "he said it again, Dad," and "one more for everyone, Dad." I was busy trying to find a way out of this mess. I wasn't going to make it through the night and was trying to formulate an exit strategy. When Ralphie finally leaves the bathroom, the bottle was finished and so was I.

In the next couple of scenes, we caught a break. Ralphie goes back to school, there is yet another dream sequence, we meet the neighbourhood bullies, and there is only one "Ralphie" just before the commercial break. Dad poured three quick ones and then headed upstairs. I confided in my big brother as we raised our glasses and steadied ourselves. "I'm not sure how much more of this I can take." He gave me a smile and a raised eyebrow.

"Don't sweat it, the bottle is done, and I think Dad is, too. I bet you he's sneaking into bed right now." My older brother leaned back into his spot on the couch, confident that he was the new king of the jungle.

Turns out the old man was just getting ready to roar. Dad walked back into the living room with a present under his arm. The commercial was over, and Ralphie was sitting at his desk waiting for the teacher to hand back his assignment covered with A-pluses. My brother and I had just downed the last of our previous shots and happily set our empty glasses on the coffee table. Dad looked at us, bewildered. "Did I miss one?"

My brother was too quick for me. "One? You missed *three* since he went back to school!" he said. Then he made me an accomplice to his lies. "Right, John?"

I really had no choice. "It's true Dad, the teacher kept calling his name. Then he had another dream sequence." I thought I was overselling it, but it worked.

Dad sat down and started opening the present. "Sorry, boys, I had to go digging under the tree for this one." Turns out the war was not over. Dad hadn't crawled off to bed, he had gone upstairs and crawled under the Christmas tree. He pulled the paper off a long rectangular box marked with the distinct Ballantine's script on the side. Dad slid the bottle out of the box with a look of reverence. "A little gift from the guys at the shop," he said as he poured out three shots of the Scotch. Dad reached for the first one, and before I could decline, he downed the second and third. Turns out the lie had worked, and this game had entered a new and dangerous territory.

Next was the famous Ralphie-says-fudge scene. It only has one "Ralphie" in it. His mother shrieks his name at him when she hears him say the word that was not *fudge*. That one drink changed the night for me. As I brought the

24

shot glass to my lips, the smell made me gag. Paul reached over and took it out of my hands. I thought he was going to escalate this stupid contest by taking a double shot. But he winked at me and poured mine out into a potted fern. My older brother may have saved my life that night, but I also remember thinking that Mom wouldn't be happy about having a booze-soaked plant in the living room.

Another commercial break and another bathroom break. This time my brother and I lined up outside in the hall as Dad went, then we took our turns, giving an awkward laugh as one person left and the next one rushed in. By the time we got back into our spots in the living room, the commercials were over, and the film was well underway again. Dad poured a round for everyone and picked up his glass, saying, "Just in case we missed one while we were upstairs" and downed his shot. My brother finished his after a pause. I made sure Dad's attention was back on the TV before I handed mine to Paul so he could water Mom's fern.

After the leg lamp is broken, Ralphie is ordered to get the glue for his father. That meant another round for us. This time pouring appeared to be harder for Dad than he had expected. He slopped a lot pouring his drink; he spilled less pouring mine and none for my brother's shot. However, he did spend an inordinate amount of time trying to aim the end of the bottle to the top of the small glass. If I remember correctly, he even had one eye closed, like he had lost confidence in his depth perception. Paul had obviously noticed this, as well. "Hey, Dad, you all right there?" Dad was quick with an answer and a smirk.

"Don't you worry about me, kiddo. I've been playing this game since college. You know, back then the guys used to call me The Hound." Then he laughed and pointed at me. "When you're older, I'll tell you what that means."

Paul came to my defence. "Dad, he's nineteen. He knows what that means."

Dad looked at me like he had never considered the idea and shrugged. "Well, okay, but don't tell your mother. She still thinks it's because I like dogs."

The fight scene with Scott Farcus is another very busy part in the movie. Ralphie is wailing on the town bully, and his little brother is calling his name. There's a couple of shots there. Then Ralphie's mother shows up and starts yelling his name, a few more shots, even the hapless victim Scott Farcus says "Ralphie" at the end. By the time the glasses had settled, the second bottle was almost done, and the fern was almost floating.

From this point on, my recollection might be a little suspect. I can firmly remember a few things. I know that in the scene where Ralphie finally gets his chance to ask Santa for the Red Ryder BB gun, we had given up on shot glasses. Either for speed or convenience or to cut down on Dad's spilling. It was straight from the bottle for the rest of the movie. It made my faking easier, but I believe it only made things worse for everyone else. At the end of the scene, we all recited the last line together — "You'll shoot your eye out, kid. Merry Christmas. Ho ho ho." When the movie hits Christmas morning, and Ralphie gets his pink bunny suit, the shots came back with a vengeance. Between his dad playing Santa with the presents — "this one's for you, Ralphie" — and his mom begging him to come down wearing the outfit that Aunt Clara had made him — "she just always gives you the nicest things, Ralphie" — it was easier for Dad to migrate to the couch to sit with us boys. Each time the dreaded name was said, the bottle was quickly passed between the three of us. Even just putting it to my lips and pretending to take a swig was rough. I was really starting to wonder how Dad was holding up when he handed the Ballantine's over to my brother and pulled out a classic Dad joke. "If they say his name much more, I think I'm going to Ralphie."

Dad wasn't a super-funny guy, but he had an endless supply of Dad jokes. Whenever I hear one or use one myself with my kids, I think of him. He was good at using them as an easy way to connect with us kids, but he was an expert at using a Dad joke to defuse a tense situation. On long car rides, Dad was quite often the best entertainment around. He could make the last long hour of a difficult drive fly by. It's like he would turn on the silly to keep us kids from driving Mom nuts. He did this thing where he would start a story and stretch it out for the remainder of the ride and never get past the beginning. "Once I knew this guy, who everyone called Charlie. Charlie wasn't his actual name. But he always wore his work coat, and in big letters on his chest there was a badge that said *Frank*. 'Hello, Frank,' they would say when they saw him. 'Good to see you, Frank.' That's what they would say when they saw him and his tractor heading through town. 'Good ol' Tractor Timmy,' they said." Dad could keep that up for hours. It would keep us enraptured for the remainder of the drive, and we'd get to Grandma's house without ever finding out what the guy's name really was. The year after we made the terrible decision to play the drinking game, Dad will cement his title as a Dad Joke Legend. When Paul brings home his college girlfriend to meet the family for the first time, they will sit awkwardly at the kitchen table, trying to think of a way to explain that she is pregnant and that they are getting married. My mom will be in shock and ask them to repeat themselves. The girlfriend, Linda, will speak for the first time that night. Linda will sheepishly reply, "I'm pregnant." Dad will then stick out his hand and say, "Nice to meet you, Pregnant. I'm George."

Eventually, the Parker family heads to the Chinese restaurant and then Ralphie heads to bed with his "blue-steel beauty" beside him in the darkness. Then the movie fades to black and the credits start to roll. With that, we all cheered, maybe a little too loudly; I'm sure we woke up Mom. We all stood up and Dad put the cap back on the bottle. He twisted it tightly, like he didn't want to risk the chance that it would be opened again any time soon.

Now, pause.

This is where the story usually ends.

When one of us is telling this story, we end it here with "Then we all stumbled to bed, swearing to never watch that movie again." It always gets a laugh, and it's a good ending, but not how it really went.

Dad was standing near the doorway, and we got up to follow him upstairs. Then he reached out to grab us both, quickly wrapping one of his big arms around each of us and pulling us in. I thought at the time he meant to pat us on the shoulders but lost his balance. I thought he was going to say something about us doing a pretty good job keeping up with the old man. That would have been more like my dad. But he just pulled us in and held on. Two big arms wrapping around his two very big little boys. Like he was trying to hold on to the memory of this moment. Through a fog of whisky and Scotch, he was trying to re-ignite the muscle memory of when he held us in his arms back when we really were little. Trying to remember what it felt like when one of his sons could fit in one of his arms. When we were so small, and he was so young.

Dad had hugged us lots growing up; he was a good father who loved his sons, and he made sure we knew it. But this time he gathered us together in his arms and squeezed us hard. He just held us. For the longest time. Then he started to cry. Sure, it could have been the booze. It could have been the emotion of the holidays. It could be having his family back together and knowing that all this was temporary. Someday, sooner than any of us wanted to admit, it would be the last time we were all together. It could have been a lot of stuff that brought this on, but he stood there and quietly sobbed with his two boys in his arms. My ear pressed to his shoulder, my arm around his back; I could feel his chest shuddering, his lungs struggling to find a steady rhythm, the low coughing sound in his throat as he tried and failed to keep it all in.

That's when I noticed Paul, my big brother, had his face buried in Dad's chest and was sobbing quietly, wrapped up in the old man's arm.

Before that night I never understood what people meant when they said "a good cry," but when Dad let us go, I felt better than I think I ever have. My tears were all done. Each one I had held inside, every tear I had pent up over the years, every tear I was holding on to was now out. I could smell the unique fatherly fragrance of cologne, sawdust, pipe smoke, and Scotch, then we all smiled and staggered to bed. The next day Mom would go to church by herself and secretly wonder what had suddenly killed all her houseplants. But that night as I laid in bed, waiting for the room to stop spinning, I thought over and over again about the last lines in that movie. The grown-up Ralphie has told us about everything from his childhood, from how to avoid bullies to the subtleties of six-year-old insult etiquette, but it was his final reflections that I will always remember.

> That Christmas would live in our memories....
> All was right with the world.
> It was the greatest Christmas gift I had ever received ... or would ever receive.
> Gradually, I drifted off to sleep.

The Christmas Divorce

WHEN PARENTS GET divorced, people say it is not the child's fault. That is true. Except in this case. The divorce *was* my fault.

When I was growing up, the Amey family was the richest family in town. Everyone knew that; it was unavoidable. As you drove into town there was a giant billboard for the father's law firm. If you missed that, the mom was always in the newspaper for donating to a charity. It seemed to be a weekly thing and always ended up with Katherine Amey's big blond hair and perfect teeth on the front page of the local newspaper. Failing that, if you still didn't know that the Amey family was the richest family in town, you could just ask one of their kids. They would tell you. Often without you asking.

Two complete brats. Spoiled-rotten rich kids with no redeeming qualities, and my mother desperately wanted us to be their friends. The daughter, Samantha, and the son, Chris, were about the same ages as me and my little sister. So, my mother saw this as the perfect chance for us to move up the social ladder of our small town. The Amey family was not only wealthy but also very influential. As my mother saw it, if my family became friends with the Ameys, it could be very beneficial. It could mean better connections for my stepfather's business. Better opportunities for school for me and my sister.

As I saw it, I would get to play with some rich kid's toys.

I don't know how we ever got invited, but my friendship with Chris Amey (the oldest child, a complete brat, spoiled-rotten rich kid with no redeeming qualities) started with a pool party. In the car on the way there, my mom laid out how everything was going to go. "Brian and I are going to be spending time with the other parents. It's important for him to meet more business people." She patted my stepfather's knee as he drove us from the poor side of town, where we lived, to the richest neighbourhood in town, where the Ameys lived. The car was a twelve-year-old station wagon that my stepdad had spent the morning washing, vacuuming, and waxing. He was a contractor, and my mom saw this as a chance to not only find more customers but better customers. Ones who would be willing to pay top dollar for his work and would have no trouble paying their bills on time. "So, you kids are going to need to spend some time with the other kids there," she said. That meant we were supposed to make friends with the Amey kids. I thought the little Amey girl was okay, as far as annoying little sisters go. Chris was a different story.

He was in my grade and no one liked him. On the grade-school playground, he was a rare breed, an outsider who was always around. There were plenty of outsiders; they were the kids who didn't play with anyone else during recess and just kept to themselves. Chris was an outsider since he didn't have any friends but was always hanging around. If we were standing around telling jokes, he would interrupt to tell us that our jokes weren't funny. If we were all playing football on Monday, he'd show up Tuesday with a brand-new football and insist we use his ball because it was so much better than the old one we had. I get it. He was a lonely rich kid trying to find a way to fit in. Doesn't mean I had to like him.

Things started as planned, for the grown-ups. Katherine Amey, wearing a sarong and bikini, greeted us at the front doors. I had never even seen a woman in a bikini who wasn't in a photograph. My mother never wore a bikini. To be honest, if you had asked, I would have said that there was a law against moms wearing bikinis. Mrs. Amey had a huge sun hat on and greeted my mom with a hug and a kiss on each cheek. Mom introduced my stepdad and then my sister and me. We all used the best manners that we had been reminded of in the car and said, "Nice to meet you," and called her Mrs. Amey. She walked us through the house toward the backyard. It was huge. Our entire house could have fit in their foyer. Our house didn't even have a foyer. It had a mudroom. The room where you took off your muddy boots before you walked through the front door and directly into our living room. As Mrs. Amey led us through the house, I stared up the main staircase. I would later learn that they did, in fact, have two sets of stairs in the house. The main one was huge and carpeted. Wide enough to drive a car up and lined with dark-oak panelling on the inside wall while giant carved spindles held the railing on the outside wall. The newel posts at the end of each flight were as wide as me and taller than my little sister. Back then I knew none of the names for the parts of a stair railing, or that the oak that was used would cost my parents a year's salary. I was only focused on one thing: getting to the pool, more specifically, the diving board.

Of course, Chris Amey had told me about his pool. He had told everyone at school about his pool. It was the biggest one in town outside the YMCA; his dad was sure about that. It was deeper than any other pool, as well; his father had made certain. The diving board was better than any other regular diving board; his father had paid extra for that. Every warm day during the school year Chris had told us about the slide and the toys and the pool that was better than any other in the city. But it was the diving board that fascinated me. I loved going off diving boards as a kid. And the Ameys' diving board was all I had thought about since Mom had told us about the invitation.

Mrs. Amey led us out through the sliding glass doors and onto the giant back deck. A bright stainless-steel barbecue to the left and a hot tub on the right. A short but wide set of stairs led you from the deck to the lawn, with a brick patio to the right and the large pool straight ahead. My mom quickly divided the group up. My little sister was introduced to Samantha, the youngest Amey. The two moms mentioned that both girls loved their dolls, and the two kids went off to play on the lawn. Mrs. Amey told my mom that she wanted to introduce my mom and stepdad to some of the people at the party. Mrs. Amey pointed toward a large group of grown-ups milling around a tiki bar. That was in the middle of the patio, in between a second barbecue and a second hot tub. Apparently, Mr. Amey didn't like having to walk upstairs for a soak or a steak. My mom pointed out that "your friend from school is right over there" and waved to Chris, who was standing by the shallow end of the pool with some other kids about our age. She nudged me toward him and headed off to the patio to schmooze her way into small town high society.

Chris was standing with a group of boys, none of whom I knew except him. They all went to a private school just outside of town. It didn't matter to me. I wasn't there to make friends; I was there to dive. It was my favourite thing to do. My sister and I took swimming lessons at the YMCA. Mom thought it was good exercise. It gave us something to do and most importantly, it was free. For me, the best part was always the last fifteen minutes of each Tuesday night lesson, free time. It was the instructor's way of getting us to pay attention. He reminded us at the beginning of each lesson that if we were good listeners, we would get fifteen minutes of free time in the pool. For most of the other kids that meant splashing around in the shallow end. Either wrestling or playing keep-away with a beach ball. For me, it meant the diving board. A long and super springy board on the deep end of the Olympic-sized pool. With a depth of sixteen feet, it was a *major* accomplishment to touch the bottom on a dive. Something none of the kids in my little dolphins group had been able to do. Most had given up trying, but not me. Every Tuesday night, as soon as the bored teenaged instructor said the words "free time," I was headed to the diving board. Touching the bottom of the pool was always the goal. I was never able to do it, but it was always fun just to try. The anticipation of waiting your turn, thinking about what you were going to do better this time — quicker steps to the launch point, a higher jump, a deeper knee bend, arms out for balance — to get the perfect arch for the perfect trajectory, then a smooth entry to propel your body down the sixteen feet to touch the bottom. Each time I got tantalizingly close as the pressure built in my ears and slowly my buoyancy grabbed hold and pulled me away from the bottom. Then back to the line at the diving board to try it all again. But not this time. There would be no fifteen-minute time limit. My mom and stepdad would be occupied for hours. They were over at the fake tiki hut with some tall brightly coloured drinks, and my little sister was sitting on a picnic blanket, rapidly switching her doll from one outfit to the next. I was free to dive all day long into the pool that Chris had bragged about so many times. All I had to do was say hi to Chris, then my best manners required that I be invited to swim before I could go into the pool. I crossed the big patch of green grass to Chris and his friends. I gave the group my biggest smile and said hi to Chris. He responded with hey and then silence. He could have introduced the other boys in the group. I could have asked their names and introduced myself. But I was only interested in the pool. After what I thought was more than enough of a pause, I tried to sound casual as I said, "So, that's the diving board you mentioned at school." Chris said yep, and that was good enough for me. I had my invitation and was off to the diving board.

Towel and shirt thrown onto a nearby lawn chair and then to the diving board I went. I can honestly say that Chris was telling the truth. It was the best diving board and the biggest pool outside of the YMCA. Whatever his father had paid for it — and I had no idea what a pool cost, I was only a kid — was worth every penny. It was just like the YMCA but better. There was no waiting. No line up, and no one behind me silently pushing for me to hurry up and dive. I could take all the time I wanted thinking about the dive. It was just a quick step to the launch point, a big jump, a deep knee bend, up into the air with arms out for balance, the perfect arch for the perfect trajectory, then a smooth entry to propel my body down to touch the bottom. Shallower than the sixteen-foot Olympic pool, I was able to touch the bottom of the pool on my first dive and quickly graduated to see how far away from the diving board I could aim and still reach the bottom. It was wonderful.

I did that same thing for hours. Over and over again. Till I was exhausted. I eventually collapsed into a lawn chair near the pool. Happy and tired. My mom came over with a paper plate full of food. Mr. Amey saw himself as a master griller and had done chicken legs, burgers, and ribs. Mom asked if I was having a good time "with my friends." I told her I was having a great time, never mentioning that I hadn't seen Chris since our "hi" and "hey" exchange from hours ago. Mom headed off to check on my sister and the little Amey girl, then back to the other grown-ups on the patio. I noticed she was a little wobbly as she walked back to the tiki hut, most likely she wasn't used to wearing her fancy shoes. I noticed she was wearing the shoes that she usually only wore on date nights.

I could not have been much happier. I basked in the sun with a plate full of food and a diving board that I had all to myself, most likely for the rest of the afternoon. I was enjoying some of Mr. Amey's ribs (he really did do a great job) when I heard my little sister arguing with Samantha Amey. Something from my sister like, "but I didn't mean to!" and then much, much louder, most likely trying to get attention, "I'm not going to play with you anymore" from the spoiled-rotten rich kid with no redeeming qualities. She then marched away from my little sister and the gathering of dolls and headed past me on her way to the pool.

I remember thinking how tiny she was as she walked by my chair. Very young. Too young to be walking around unsupervised. She passed the end of my lounger as I put down my cob of corn and reached for the hamburger. She stomped her tiny little feet over to the assortment of toys lying beside the pool and picked out an inflatable ring. It was obviously hers, small, with little stars on it. Probably from a TV show that she and my sister both loved. She stepped into it, pulled it up to her waist, and jumped feet first into the pool. Immediately sinking to the bottom of the pool, which was only a little less deep than the local YMCA pool. When she hit the water, her bottom half sank till the ring touched the surface. Then the floating ring did what floating rings do: it floated, quickly lifting the little girl's arms above her head as she continued down, while the ring stayed floating on the surface. She was at the bottom of the pool. I was eating a hamburger. I wish I could say that I immediately sprang into action like a preteen *Baywatch* lifeguard, but I just took another bite. In my mind I was asking, *Did anyone else see her go under? Someone is going to help her, right?* So, I waited. I finished my mouthful (Mr. Amey really had done a great job on the barbecuing) and then dove into the pool. My technique was perfect. The practice had really paid off. I had the perfect angle as I stepped off the edge of the pool and launched myself downward. I can still clearly see the confused look on Samantha's face. Like when you walk into a room and can't remember why you had gone in there. I grabbed her right arm and swam for the surface.

When we reached the top of the water, there were grown-ups screaming. Apparently, her parents had noticed her sitting at the bottom of the pool, but only after I dove in. Her father grabbed the girl out of my arms and lifted her out of the water, then her crying mother grabbed the girl from her father. Samantha spit up a bunch of water, and then she was crying, too. My mother pushed through the gathered crowd of grown-ups and grabbed me in a very tight hug. She pushed my hair aside and looked closely at my face as she asked if I was all right. One of the nearby dads answered for me, "Of course he's all right. The kid's a hero!" He started to clap. The other parents joined in, and then Mr. and Mrs. Amey turned their attention to me. Mr. Amey grabbed me by my shoulder and said, "Thanks, hero." I smiled, feeling pretty proud. Mrs. Amey was still crying and screaming when she grabbed me and hugged me. I was still feeling very proud, but being this close to my first bikini, my pride was mixed up with a lot of other very confusing feelings.

From the moment that I "saved Samantha's life," (her parents' words, not mine) Chris and I started spending a lot more time together. Our parents kept arranging "play-dates" for us, and they would hang out and gossip while I got to play with the rich kid's toys. I loved every moment. Not being with Chris. No amount of toys could stop him from being a spoiled-rotten rich kid with no redeeming qualities. But he had the best toys and the best house. The best toys because he had so many that they occupied the entire top floor of the house. His parents had converted the servants' quarters into a massive playroom. Knocking down the walls between the rooms that at one time had been the living quarters for the butler and the maid as well as a shared den and a small kitchenette. The parents filled this massive room with toys. I thought it was paradise. Chris always seemed bored with his toys, no matter how many he had.

The house was fantastic, too. Not only did it have servants' quarters turned into a playroom, but the servants had their own staircase. A narrow and undecorated staircase that was built into the back of the house. Instead of going straight from one floor to the next, it criss-crossed the back of the house. The idea was that the servants could use the staircase to access every room in the house without ever having to use the main stairs and possibly interfere with the owners of the house. For the original owners of the home, it was a way to avoid the servants; for me and Chris, it was a way to play the ultimate game of hide and seek. Using the front stairs or the back stairs, the hider could go anywhere in the house while the seeker counted. Then, if you were hiding and the seeker got too close, there was always an escape. You could move from one room to another with ease. Even better, the old mansion had lots of squeaky wooden floors. The effect was perfect; if the house was quiet enough, or you were close enough, you could hear when your opponent was on the move. It was wonderful, but it got even better in the mideighties when the Nerf Blaster was invented.

Like every kid watching Saturday morning cartoons, I saw the commercial and asked my parents to buy me the Nerf gun in the ad. My mom smiled and gave me a very clear answer: "Well, let's see if it's on your Christmas list in a few months." What she meant was "if you're still interested in it in November, you can put it on your Christmas list and then I'll think about it if it isn't too expensive." I was old enough to know that there was a slim chance I would ever get one for Christmas. But I was old enough to know that Chris Amey only had to ask, and he would get as many Nerf Blasters as he wanted. All he needed to do was ask. And all I needed to do was make sure he asked.

The next day at school, I didn't mention it to him, but I did mention it to everyone else. Of course, every one of my friends had seen the commercial. Of course, every one of my friends had asked their parents. No one got one. We were each told one of two things: that we should save our allowance, or we could ask for it at Christmastime. When Chris came over to hover around my friends at recess, Nerf Blasters were all anyone was talking about. From the practical: Who was most likely to get on for Christmas? How long would you have to save your allowance? To the imaginative: How would we divide the teams when we all got to play? Which park would be the best place to play? Chris didn't participate much in the conversation, but I knew it had paid off when I was invited for another playdate a few days later.

Our Nerf battles lasted all day. Chris and I chased each other from floor to floor as our moms gossiped and drank white wine. The old house creaked and groaned, making it seem like the person hunting you was always just around the next corner. We ran up and down stairwells, jumped over custom-made couches, and hid behind antique cabinets, launching bullets behind us as we ran. Never once worried about hitting one of the original oil paintings or any of the large one-of-a-kind chandeliers that hung throughout the house. We only stopped when my mother announced that it was time to go home. Then Chris did something I had never seen. He gave his mother heck. It was astounding. He sounded just like my mom as he spoke to his mom. Let's say I forgot to do a chore. My mother would always say the same thing. She'd say, "What were you thinking? Did you think at all that someone else was now going to have to do your chore?" And then she'd say, "Why do I have to be the one who does everything?" That was her three-pronged attack whenever she was giving me heck. But Chris was using this same technique on his mom. Because each Nerf gun came with twenty darts, we were constantly pausing the battle to go around and collect darts.

"Why would you only get a couple of darts for each gun? What were you thinking?" As Chris started to berate his mother, my mother began shuffling me toward the front door. "Did you think at all that now Dad is going to have to go and get more darts?" My mom was handing me my coat and pushing me out the front door. I was dragging my feet, in awe of what Chris was doing and wondering what the secret was to be able to talk to a parent like that.

Mrs. Amey was smiling directly at my mom and telling Chris, "We'll talk about this later" over and over again.

"I mean they make it in a pack of one hundred. Why wouldn't you just grab two of those? Why do I have to be the one who thinks of everything?" I was watching the whole scene with my mouth hanging open, sure that he was about to get yelled at or sent to his room or grounded, but the opposite happened.

Before Mrs. Amey closed the door she said in a reassuring voice, "Chris, I'll pick some up tomorrow. I'm sorry." I remember thinking that he must be the luckiest kid in the world. It was strange that he was always so sad.

We forgot about the Nerf battles after Chris's father returned from a business trip to Japan. Suddenly, the toy room was filled with giant animal robots. Each one came preassembled and had eyes that lit up as soon as you touched the top of their head. There were three different kinds of robot dogs, a dangerous-looking robo-snake, and one thing that looked like it was half monkey and half cat. They were fascinating to look at, with smooth sleek lines and cool-sounding whirs and buzzes as they moved their heads or beaks or zipped around the room on hidden rubber wheels. But we could never get them to do anything. At least not what we thought they were supposed to do. See, the Japanese instructions were useless to us, but the illustrations made us think they could do really cool tricks. If we were interpreting the illustrations correctly, the dogs could talk to each other and then they would play follow-the-leader as they walked in a figure eight and sang a song. While they would bark a little when you turned them on, they would never move, no matter what we did. We did get a lot of laughs out of playing with those dogs because after a few seconds, a male voice would come out of a speaker under one of the dog's tails and say something in Japanese that sounded to us like "donkey seated, donkey seated." We thought it was hilarious. A deep male voice booming out of a small plastic robot dog's butt, and all it could say was "donkey seated, donkey seated." Chris would turn on the dogs just so he could ask, "Is the donkey sitting down?" And when the Japanese man answered back, we howled laughing.

The robot snake never danced; the robot cat never pounced; the robot fox would not pick up its robot bone. The only one that we could make move was the owl. The biggest of the bunch at a foot and a half tall, it was very impressive. Even though it never did what we saw in the instructions. Turn it on, and it would come to life. Clicking its beak, turning its robot head side to side with the sound of whirring motors. Then it would make a low sound of an internal servo as it slowly raised and lowered its wings. The issue was that if the illustrations were to be believed, we were supposed to be able to use the flute that came in the box to control how the owl moved. The pictures seemed to show that playing different notes on the flute would make the big robot owl turn left or right or move forward or even spin. The problem was that the owl never seemed to do what you wanted. If the picture in the instructions showed that covering the third hole on the flute would make the owl spin, then Chris's owl would turn left. Blow the same note, and it would turn right. Blow the same note again, and it would spin around and chirp. It was frustrating, but I was not ready to give up. I wanted to keep testing and trying to figure out how to control the expensive new toy. Chris had a better idea. "I'd rather tell it to jump off the stairs." We locked eyes, he grabbed the robot, and we headed for the top of the wide oak staircase.

The game was simple. You had five whistles to get the owl to fall down the stairs. Then it was the other person's turn. Since we never figured out control of the toy it was just random to see when the robot owl was going to lose this game of chicken with three flights of stairs. Both of us would take our turn as the robot skated along the top of the stairs. Sometimes retreating from the edge and moving farther back than when we had first started this game. On other turns, the owl would bolt for the top stair, only to stop with one wheel hanging over the edge to whistle and chirp and click its beak. Chris was the one who finally got it to drop over the edge of the stair. Only fair since it was his very expensive, brand-new imported toy we were trying to destroy. It was almost at the end of his turn when the owl turned around to put its back to the stairs. We were both disappointed knowing that he had only one blow on the flute left, and our victim was now facing the wrong way. Chris gave it one last whistle as he handed the flute to me, and the owl raced backward off the top step and out of sight. We were shocked. None of the illustrations had shown how to get the owl to move backward, and it had never once shown us that it could do that. We ran to the railing as the robot bounced off the third stair down and sprung up into the air. A few more bounces on the way down and the owl started to whistle and chirp as it crashed, making us laugh at the idea that the owl was very happy to be thrown down a flight of stairs. When it made the first of the two landings, it slammed into the wall and headed down the second flight, and at this point pieces started to fly off. First a wing, then part of its tail, then an eye came loose, holding on by some exposed wires. Its momentum slammed it into a few more stairs and a spindle or two as it reached the ground floor. Just before it came to rest, missing a lot of pieces at the bottom of the huge staircase, the man's voice came back. This time it sounded like "hey there, buddy." Like a small Japanese man was trapped inside the owl and was asking the owl to be more careful. "Hey there, buddy. I'm stuck in here, and I can't see what's going on, but it felt like we just went backward down three flights of stairs. Could you be a little more careful next time?" The game changed from trying to get the owl to fall down to the stairs to trying to get the little Japanese guy to say, "Hey there, buddy."

After the first trip down the stairs, the owl became much easier to control. Not control exactly. We still had no ability to guide the toy, but it did go down the stairs much faster. As if the owl had accepted its fate. After about six or eight whistles the owl seemed to give up and just hurl itself off the edge. We'd stand at the top watching it smash and crash its way down the vintage hardwood stairway, waiting for the little man to say his Japanese catchphrase. Then we'd repeat it back when he did, yelling, "Hey there, buddy" over the railing at him as he begged for the ride to stop. It was funny every time, and the robot owl survived most of the afternoon.

The next day at school I wondered out loud to Chris how we were able to destroy one of his toys without any form of punishment. He told me that he was punished, and then explained his parents' sticker system. The system was quite simple in design. In the two months leading up to Christmas, Mr. and Mrs. Amey would set aside a strip of stickers for each child. On October 25th, each child started with ten stickers. Good behaviour meant that the child got extra stickers, and bad behaviour meant that stickers were taken away. Then at Christmas time, each sticker represented one present. Simple, and it seemed to be a very effective way to get a child to behave. At least in theory. I asked Chris what he had to do to lose or gain a sticker. That is when I realized the reality of the situation.

Chris explained that he never really lost any stickers. If he did get in trouble, and his father took away some of his stickers, all he needed to do to get them back was wait. Chris used the example of his report card. Just before the Christmas break, Chris brought home his report card and his dad was really upset, even though, as Chris said, "It really wasn't that bad." So, his father went to the big corkboard in the kitchen where the stickers were tacked to the wall and unpinned three of the stickers. He put them back in the cupboard above the sink and reminded Chris that he would have to work very hard if he wanted to earn them back.

The next day his mother called him into the kitchen and gave him the stickers back. She said it was for getting along with his little sister so well recently, but Chris didn't remember doing anything special; his mom just felt guilty about him losing stickers. I don't think my mom ever felt guilty about one of my punishments. She always said, "This is harder on me than it is you." But not once did I get the impression that it actually was hard on her. Even better, Chris explained that as they got closer to Christmas, his mom would just start handing out stickers for nothing. As long as his dad wasn't around, all Chris had to do was wait for more stickers and more presents. Just when I thought his life couldn't get any better, he explained why his family didn't make a list for Santa. Instead, he and his sister went on a shopping spree! Maybe his parents hated lists or didn't want to bother mailing a letter to Santa, but his parents just took them to the toy store and let them get whatever they wanted. I was more than a little skeptical, so I asked him to walk me through each step.

A week before Christmas his whole family would drive to the toy store. His mom and dad would give him and his little sister the stickers that they had "earned" over the last two months. Then they would walk through the toy store, placing stickers on the shelves of the toys that they wanted. When all the stickers were placed, the kids headed off to wait in the car while their mom and dad walked the aisles again, picking up each and every choice. Everything would be wrapped and loaded in the back of the family vehicle to be transported home and opened on Christmas morning.

It sounded unbelievable, but I had seen the way he spoke to his mother. It kind of made it seem like the normal rules of childhood did not apply in his house. Besides, I was too excited to worry about the truth. I had a plan.

First, I needed to know the rules. Any toy you wanted? He said, "Yes, sometimes, if a toy is really expensive, then my dad will say that it costs two stickers. Like one time, when I was little, I wanted a ride-on Jeep. He said that one was two stickers." Okay, what about multiples of one toy? "Yeah, one time I wanted to get two boxes of army men, so I put two stickers on the shelf, and I got two boxes for Christmas." Finally, how many stickers will you get? "I don't know," he said, and shrugged. "Last year I only got eleven, but the year before I got like sixteen." That was all I needed to know. My plan would work. Now I needed to convince Chris to go along with it.

I laid out the idea at the next play date. The perfect combination of the sticker system and the massive toy room gave Chris a unique opportunity. I presented him with a page I had cut out of the Christmas catalogue. Some big glossy pictures and a snappy summary under the title "Tyco International Pro Racing Slot Car Set." The ad said it was an "exciting slot car racing with the world's fastest cars with fifty-four feet of tack, including a figure eight and two loops." I started Chris off gently, first just asking if he had seen this ad in the catalogue. He said he had but wasn't really interested in slot cars. That could have been the end of my plan right there, but I pressed on. Focusing instead on what the Tyco International could do that other slot car sets could not. I pointed to one of the highlighted areas on the left side of the ad. "Yeah, I'm not crazy about them, either. But this thing looks cool. See, in the straight-away there is an automatic lane changer, that way no car has the inside lane for the whole race. Makes it fair. Plus, if both cars reach the lane changer at the same time, they crash." I knew we were both thinking of the fun of watching an imported robot owl jack-knife off the top of the stairs. Now that I had his attention, I pressed on with my plan. "Plus, it comes with a lap counter that keeps track of who is winning. So, there could be no cheating. We could say the first one to do twenty laps wins —"

"Or a super long race, first one to finish one-hundred laps," he interrupted. I knew I had him hooked. He took the catalogue page out of my hand and started examining the accessories. "Oh, check this out," he said. "It has a speaker built into the grandstand. Says here that it plays cheering crowd noises and car sounds as you drive. So cool. I could put one sticker on the racetrack and put one sticker on the grandstand." I had him. He was in the car, now all

I had to do was drive him to the final destination. I recited the line that I had been practising, "Now it says fifty-four feet of track, what if, and I know this sounds crazy, what if you got two tracks? That's one-hundred-and-eight feet of track, and it would only cost you two stickers." I stepped back from him; he was staring down at the catalogue page. I was thinking I had pushed him too far too soon.

Then he looked up and said, "What about three sets?" I was no longer at the steering wheel. He was driving, and we were hitting speeds I had never even dreamed possible.

We settled on five sets. Plus all the accessories. The grandstand, the lane changer, the lap counter, and even the limited-edition cars with working headlights so we could race in the dark. Together it was going to be two-hundred-and-sixteen feet of track winding and looping its way through the converted servants' quarters. A number that, I'll be honest, was hard for us to calculate and actually required Chris to get out his math textbook to make sure we were doing the multiplication correctly. We walked through each step of the plan. Where we would put the turns and the loops. Who would get the inside track first, and how would count down the start of the race. We were still daydreaming out loud when it was time for me to go home. With the Christmas break starting tomorrow, I wasn't going to see him again until after Christmas day when he would have a slot-car racetrack bigger than I had ever even imagined. It was so close I could almost see the cars zipping around the toy room. I wanted to make sure everything was set. "Okay, are you sure you know what you need to do?" I asked.

He replied, "Yes, no wait, what do I need to do?"

I tried to sound reassuring. I smiled and said, "All you need to do is be good." Then I remembered that the normal kid rules didn't apply. "Or don't," I stammered, "I'm not sure. Just make sure you have at least eight stickers when you go to the toy store."

Christmas in my house came and went. I did enjoy it, but whenever there was a quiet moment, I found myself daydreaming about Chris's slot-car track. Did he have it all set up yet? How fast did the cars go? Did he set up the loops in a big row or spread them out around the room? It was a few days before my mom told me we were going to see the Ameys. It took a lot longer for us to get the invitation than I had thought it would.

Once in the door of the mansion, I raced up the stairs to see the track — oh, and Chris. Three flights of stairs as fast as I could run. Stumbling more than once in my excitement. Only to find Chris alone in the room, surrounded by Transformers. I asked what had happened at the toy store. Chris said that it was a disaster. He had followed the plan: five stickers on the shelf with the tracks, one more on each of the accessories. Then off to the car with his sister. When his mom and dad figured out what Chris had done, his dad was very mad. He was marching back to the car when they stopped outside the door of the toy store. There was shouting and pointing, and then more shouting until Mr. Amey left in a taxi and Mrs. Amey drove home crying.

By the start of the new year, Mr. Amey was sharing an apartment with one of the secretaries at his work. When I heard my mom tell the story, it sounded like he had owned the apartment for a long time and the secretary already had a key, which was convenient. By the summer, the guy who cleaned the Amey's pool had moved into their house. I guessed with Mr. Amey gone, Mrs. Amey needed to have her pool cleaned a little more often. So, I guess it was a good idea to have someone there full time.

Looking back on the situation, I still can't help but feel that in some small way, this might have been my fault.

Merry Christmas, Mr. Baggins

THIS IS A story about a great Christmas story. And like any great Christmas story, this story that takes me back to the happiest days of my childhood makes me think about my family and reminds me of all the important things of the season.

The story is *The Hobbit* by J.R.R. Tolkien.

See, for my family, listening to the Tolkien classic was one of our holiday traditions. It went hand in hand with another, much more common holiday tradition: a very, very long drive to my grandparents' house. Each year, as soon as my older sisters and I were out of school, Mom and Dad would pack us into the family car and begin the long drive to the town where my father grew up. My dad's mother and father still lived there. Each Christmas we made the annual trek to visit them. Me, Dad, Mom, and two annoying sisters driving for thirty-six hours.

Mom did her best with the situation, always calling it "our adventure." Never "two straight days of driving in poor weather to visit people who still blamed her for making their son move so far away." Nope, as she did with everything, Mom made the best of it. She prepared by packing snacks and marking restaurants on the map. She would bring travel games and books and would be the one to start the licence plate game and I Spy.

She was the one in charge of the kids; Dad was in charge of driving. Mom only drove if Dad was asleep. Dad's contribution to keeping peace in the car was heading to the library before the drive and getting some books on tape. That was his only job. That and repeatedly telling us to be quiet and listen to the story.

Mom was the sheriff of the back seat, and as sheriff, she was the one who decided where each child sat. Within the old family Ford, seat position was extremely important. The best spot was behind Mom — not only was she smaller than Dad, but she was also willing to put up with less leg room to preserve the peace in the back seat. Sitting behind her felt like riding in a limousine. This spot was almost always taken by my oldest sister.

Dad was a big guy, so sitting behind the driver meant zero leg room. The space was cramped so badly that it meant the child who got this spot spent most of the drive cross-legged. Yes, thirty-six hours without your feet being able to touch the floor. But that was only the second-worst spot. The worst spot in the back seat was always mine. It was called The Bump. The tiny, under-padded space that sat between the two back seats. The positioning of the driveshaft of the old Ford made a large lump in the vehicle's interior running from bumper to bumper. In the rest of the car, it made no difference but in the spot that I occupied for the majority of the three-day journey, it made every minute torturous. The poorly placed driveshaft meant I sat with my knees folded and my feet level with my seat. The so-called seat was about half an inch of cloth, which hid the metal chassis. The space was about half the width of a human torso, with a protruding lump in the middle that made sitting comfortably simply impossible. Occupying The Bump was like sitting cross-legged on a saddle. Small, uncomfortable, and devoid of an armrest, that is where the youngest child remained for the majority of the trip. Make no mistake, the person who designed this vehicle was not incompetent, no. He knew exactly what he was doing. He just hated kids.

It was on one of these very long drives, very late one night, that a small miracle occurred. My mom was done driving for the night and wanted to sleep in the back. Since I was the only kid still awake, Dad asked if I would like to ride up front so Mom could get in the back and get some rest. Mom pulled into the gas station and switched to the back seat. I climbed right over the back of the passenger seat and bounced into the front beside Dad. The amount of room was amazing. I could stretch my legs all the way without hitting the dash. The seat was plush and soft and at least three times the size of the spot I had been occupying since we started out that morning. I instantly began touching every button I could reach and flipping the silver ashtray lid up and down. At least until Dad pointed and said, "Cool it." I put on my seatbelt and smiled so Dad would know that I wasn't about to make trouble.

Dad and I drove in silence for a little, and whenever I started talking, he put his fingers to his lips and pointed a thumb at the back seat. Now that I have kids of my own, I know that Dad's plan was just to wait me out until I fell asleep. I was only eight, so I should have nodded off within twenty minutes. But now that I have kids of my own, I know that they only sleep when you need them awake, and the more you need them to sleep, the longer they stay awake. Sitting in the front was just too exciting. I asked Dad about the signs we passed. I asked him if he was watching out for deer like the last sign said. I asked him if he was watching out for moose like the other sign said. I asked him if he had ever seen a sign that said watch out for moose and deer. I thought I was being helpful. Now that I have kids of my own, I know that nothing is less helpful than a child who is trying to be helpful.

After thirty minutes or so of my "helping" Dad drive, he was forced to pull out his only contribution to the entertainment for the thirty-six-hour drive. His books on tape. I remember picking through the plastic cases to find something we both liked. It was mostly kid stuff and Christmas stories. Nancy Drew for my sisters and at least one telling of "'Twas the Night Before Christmas." But when I read the title *The Hobbit*, my dad was enthusiastic, saying it was his favourite and it was the first real book he had ever read. He put in the first of six tapes and told me that if I felt sleepy, I could just close my eyes and he would wake me up when we stopped for breakfast. Now that I have kids of my own, I know what he meant was, "Please go to sleep."

But I never did. I stayed awake for the full three hours and thirty-five minutes. From the small hobbit hole in the Shire all the way to the Lonely Mountain and back again. I listened to a calm, smooth English accent read the unabridged version of the book. As each side of the tape ended, Dad whispered, "Are you still awake?" And when I answered yes, he recapped the storyline to make sure I was able to follow along. I had never heard a story like this one, and I had never seen my dad so excited about a book.

After the chapter called "Roast Mutton," Dad paused before putting in the second tape. He made sure I understood the simple brilliance of keeping the trolls arguing until the sun rose and turned them to stone.

> William never spoke for he stood turned to stone as he stooped; and Bert and Tom were stuck like rocks as they looked at him. And there they stand to this day, all alone, unless the birds perch on them; for trolls, as you probably know, must be underground before dawn, or they go back to the stuff of the mountains they are made of, and never move again. That is what had happened to Bert and Tom and William.

Then, before hitting play on the next tape, my dad made sure to hype up the moment when Bilbo meets the elves of Rivendell. He did that same thing in between each tape and sometimes paused in the middle of the story to make sure I understood what was going on. As our car wound along deep dark roads, it was very easy for a small child to imagine the party of dwarves as they headed toward the home of the lord of Rivendell, Elrond.

> Bilbo never forgot the way they slithered and slipped in the dusk down the steep zig-zag path into the secret valley of Rivendell. The air grew warmer as they got lower, and the smell of the pine-trees made him drowsy, so that every now and again he nodded and nearly fell off, or bumped his nose on the pony's neck. Their spirits rose as they went down and down. The trees changed to beech and oak, and there was a comfortable feeling in the twilight. The last green had almost faded out of the grass, when they came at length to an open glade not far above the banks of the stream.

Especially during the chapter "Riddles in the Dark," when Bilbo and Gollum play their deadly game of riddles, Dad stopped the tape each time to give me a chance to answer. I never got a single one of them, but Dad always gave me clues before he pressed play again. I remember being so impressed with the answer each time. When Gollum guessed "teeth," or Bilbo answered "wind," or when Bilbo responded with the answer "dark," and Gollum finally answered "egg." I was impressed with how smart the characters were and how quickly they answered.

Then Gollum thought the time had come to ask something hard and horrible. This is what he said:

> *This thing all things devours:*
> *Birds, beasts, trees, flowers;*
> *Gnaws iron, bites steel;*
> *Grinds hard stones to meal;*
> *Slays king, ruins town,*
> *And beats high mountain down.*

We travelled down long stretches of dark, empty highway while the hobbit, the wizard, and the thirteen dwarves travelled to the mountain of Erebor. I can't honestly say I was able to follow the whole story; I was maybe a little young for this book. But I do remember a lot about listening to *The Hobbit*.

Mostly I remember my dad. His deep and rough voice as he whispered the summary of each part of the story before flipping over the tape. The excitement on his face when he talked about the Battle of the Five Armies. The way he tried to sound like the English narrator when he said "Glóin" and "Gandalf." I remember the way he would smile out toward the road when he talked with me about what had just happened in the story. I remember the only time that night when he stopped the tape so he could rewind it. It was the description of the dragon. My dad kept one hand on the wheel while he rewound the cassette so he could hear Smaug boasting to the little hobbit again:

"My armour is like tenfold shields, my teeth are swords, my claws spears, the shock of my tail is a thunderbolt, my wings a hurricane, and my breath death!"

When the tapes were all done, when chapter nineteen was finished, when Bilbo had made his way back to Bag End, my dad and I stayed up talking for the rest of the night. Dad basically told me the entire story of *The Lord of the Rings* while occasionally telling me that I needed to get some sleep and that if Mom saw that I was still awake, we were both going to get in trouble. But it never happened. Mom slept through the night, and we talked about dwarves and elves and rings until morning.

When we stopped for breakfast, everyone in the back seat assumed I had been asleep like them. But I hadn't been. I had been with my dad to Middle Earth. We had gone on an adventure together: we defeated a dragon, found the Arkenstone, and made Dáin the king under the mountain. Just the two of us. My sisters hadn't been to Beorn's house. My mother hadn't gone to see the cave palace of the elven king. Just we did that. Just me and my dad.

We stopped at a small place called Tina's. I don't know if Tina's Restaurant still exists. The world has changed so much since then. I really doubt it is still around. But I can tell you this: if it is still open, it hasn't changed at all. Not since it was first decorated in the late fifties with a dead-animals-hung-on-every-wall motif. If Tina's is still there, then there is a huge trout on a plaque above the men's bathroom door. The huge fish is just to the left of the "no smoking" sign, so, of course, someone put a cigarette in its mouth.

When we settled into our booth at Tina's, I think a little sleep deprivation kicked in, and I think it was quickly apparent to my mom and sisters. Dad and I spent the entire breakfast saying good morning to each other. The two of us, on either end of the *U*-shaped booth, speaking in bad English accents, trying to sound like Bilbo and Gandalf when they meet at the very beginning of the book. "Good morning, I'll have the pancakes." "Good morning, pass the toast." "Good morning, can I have more orange juice?" Good morning. Good morning. Good morning. Good morning. We "good morning-ed" until my mom had had enough. She told us to stop it, and we just did it more. I think that is why it stuck. We "good morning-ed" 'cause it was funny, and we "good morning-ed" 'cause it was forbidden. And most important to me, we "good morning-ed" 'cause just the two of us, no one else, knew what we were talking about or why it made us laugh so hard.

We listened to *The Hobbit* the next night, both nights on the return journey, and several times each trip in the following years.

Now, my kids and I have watched the movies together several times over the years. We watched the cartoon when they were young. I read my boys the book as their bedtime story. But it was never the same as when my dad and I listened to the old audio cassettes while travelling in the family station wagon. The darkness always just beyond the reach of the headlights, my dad's hands looking impossibly large on the steering wheel, the quiet hiss of the tape whenever the narrator took a pause. It was magic. A young boy, his father, and the quest to reclaim the kingdom of Erebor.

That's why I'm recording this. I hope you hear it as I did. Just you and your dad. The two of you together to defeat the dragon, avenge the fallen king, and reclaim what is yours. Merry Christmas, grandson.

Chapter I: AN UNEXPECTED PARTY

In a hole in the ground there lived a hobbit. Not a nasty, dirty, wet hole, filled with the ends of worms and an oozy smell, nor yet a dry, bare, sandy hole with nothing in it to sit down on or to eat: it was a hobbit-hole, and that means comfort.

The Pigeon King Saves Christmas

BEFORE I BEGIN, there are a few things you need to know about pigeons. First, the leader of the flock is called the Pigeon King. The Pigeon King has three responsibilities. He has to make sure that his flock has a warm, dry place to live; he must keep the flock safe; and he must make sure the flock has plenty of food. The second thing you need to know is that no pigeon has ever celebrated Christmas. Yes, pigeons do have celebrations, but they don't have calendars. You've never seen a pigeon nest with a calendar pinned to the wall. You've never seen a pigeon fly by carrying a small day planner. Pigeon celebrations don't occur every year or every month. Pigeon celebrations occur naturally and spontaneously. Like when a pigeon spots a piece of bread left behind at a picnic, that would be as exciting as, say, the first day of summer vacation. Or when a pigeon is alone in a park, and an old lady arrives with a bag of breadcrumbs.

To a pigeon, that would be like their birthday. Or if a truck full of bread rolls over and all the bread spills out all over the road. That would be like a New Year's Eve party. I should also let you know that pigeons really like bread. But they don't like Christmas; to them it is just another day. So, it was just another day to the Pigeon King when he flew over the Holiday Train.

The Holiday Train is a beautifully decorated train that goes from town to town spreading Christmas cheer. It is covered with thousands of Christmas lights, from the tip of the engine to the tail of the caboose, and it brings a giant party to every town that it stops in. As the Holiday Train approaches each new town, the kids see the colourful glow of the train's lights in the distance and start to cheer. They know that when the train stops, the party will start. Out of the train will pour tons of people carrying huge piles of food. There will be free popcorn, cotton candy, cake and cookies, hot chocolate, hot apple cider, candy canes, and even marshmallows for roasting. Along with the amazing food there will be lots of entertainment. There are marching bands, jugglers, circus clowns, face painters, stilt walkers, and even a magician.

It was actually the magician who explained all this. The magician was not really talking to the Pigeon King. The magician was talking to one of the jugglers from the train. The magician was a young boy who went by the very impressive name of the Amazing Justin Papano.

His final trick of the show was "the disappearing milk trick." It was the one where he rolled up a newspaper into a cone and poured milk into it, then crushed the paper into a ball and showed the audience that the milk had disappeared. Then he would roll the newspaper back into a cone and pour out a full glass of milk.

It was amazing, and the crowds always loved it. It was an especially good trick when the audience had just finished eating their cookies. The cookies were the part that caught the Pigeon King's attention.

The Pigeon King, as I said, had three jobs as king. He had been able to find his flock a safe place for the winter, a large building with a good roof and lots of space in the rafters for nests. The Pigeon King had also been able to keep his flock safe. Recently, he had been able to remove one of the most dangerous things in the neighbourhood. There was a local dog who always barked at the Pigeon King's flock as they flew over the backyard where the noisy dog lived. The Pigeon King had noticed one day that the dog's owners had left the gate to the backyard open. The Pigeon King had flown down, staying just out of reach of the angry dog, and led the dog out of the yard and down the street to the woods outside of town. That is where the Pigeon King soared away and left the dog. Lost in the woods far from home. Sure, the dog would eventually find his way home, but the Pigeon King thought that by then the dog would have learned some manners and would not bother defenceless pigeons who weren't hurting anyone.

But the third job of the Pigeon King was to find his flock food. And lately, that had been very tough. This winter was very cold and very windy. So, the little old ladies who normally fed his flock at the park were staying home.

The old men who filled the bird feeders in their backyards had been forgetting their duties. The clumsy children who brought bags of chips to the playground were busy spilling their snacks inside, where the Pigeon King and his flock could not get them.

So, when the Amazing Justin Papano started talking about the food that was headed to the next town, the Pigeon King knew that he needed to learn more. He flew to a spot high up under an overhang where he could keep a watchful eye on the train and at the same time keep tabs on the Amazing Justin Papano. Justin headed away to find a magic shop so he could stock up on squirting flowers and smoke bombs before the train left for the next show.

The plan was simple. Find out where the train was headed. Fly back and get the flock. Watch the kids spill popcorn and cookies all night. Then the pigeons would feast. It was the perfect plan.

Then the squirrels showed up.

There are a few things that you should know about squirrels. First, they are very mischievous. That doesn't mean that they are bad, just a little naughty. Squirrels like going places and doing things that maybe they shouldn't. They don't think about the consequences of their actions. Squirrels might think they are having harmless fun when really they are causing a lot of trouble. The second thing you need to know about squirrels is that pigeons and squirrels have a tense relationship. The two groups are friendly, but they often compete. They are often looking to live in the same trees. They are often looking to use the same sticks for their nests. They are often looking to eat the same breadcrumbs thrown by the same old lady. Also, just like pigeons, squirrels really like bread.

The Pigeon King was watching from this perch when the first of the squirrels came out of the woods and climbed onto the Holiday Train. He went right to one of the bright Christmas lights and started to investigate. The squirrel sniffed it, then poked it with a paw, then licked it to see if he could eat it. If the squirrel had stopped there, the pigeons and the squirrels could have avoided a lot of trouble. But the squirrel started to turn the light bulb. He twisted it twice and the bright red light came out into his mischievous little paws. The squirrel thought that turning off the first light was neat, but he thought the second one was funny, and the third one was hilarious. After he untwisted the fourth one, he called his friends over to see what he had discovered. One after another the squirrels came out of the woods and learned the secret to turning off the lights. They would twist the bulbs and laugh when the lights turned off. Then they would call more friends from the woods, who would come and turn off even more lights. The army of squirrels made quick work of the train. Before long, all of the light bulbs had been taken out and were sitting in the snowbanks on either side of the train tracks.

By the time the giant engine started up, all the lights were out, and piles of squirrels were rolling around in the snow, laughing and holding their stomachs.

The Amazing Justin Papano was back from the magic shop and was boarding the train when he noticed the lights. He tried to explain to the conductor that they need-ed to try to fix the lights before leaving for the next town.

But the conductor wouldn't hear of it. "We've got a schedule to keep. If we don't leave now, we will be running late all week. Besides, the lights aren't that important. Now let's go, Mr. Amazing Jason Po-po-no. We have a schedule to keep."

The young magician begged the conductor to understand what the lights meant to the families in the cities. "The lights on the Holiday Train are the most important thing. The lights signal to all the boys and girls that the Christmas party is coming. The lights are their invitation. If they don't see the lights coming down the track, they won't know that they are invited to the party. They won't be there for the jugglers or the clowns or the marching bands or the hot chocolate or the popcorn or the cookies."

It was this last part that caught the Pigeon King's attention. No lights meant no kids. No kids meant no food. No food meant no crumbs. No crumbs meant the flock would go hungry. The Pigeon King needed to do something to get those lights back on.

The Amazing Justin Papano was unpacking his bags of magic supplies, and the Pigeon King landed on top of the caboose. Then the engine of the Holiday Train came to life. The engineer was shovelling coal into the firebox and white wisps of smoke started to rise out of the smokestack. The Pigeon King would need to hurry.

At first, the Pigeon King thought he could just fly the light bulbs back and forth from the snowbanks to the train and put the bulbs back in by himself. But then he realized this wasn't an option. His bird body was great for lots of things. His talons were great for picking up French fries; his beak was wonderful at picking up pizza crusts; his wings were perfect for soaring over parking lots. But his talons were no good at picking up little light bulbs; his beak was not very useful for twisting things; his wings were majestic but couldn't hold the tiny lights.

He needed a new plan. He stood on the roof of the train and glared back at the gang of squirrels playing and laughing in the snow. That's when it hit him: they had paws. Paws that can take light bulbs out are paws that can put light bulbs back in. He would have to persuade the squirrels to help him.

The Pigeon King flew back to the squirrels and spotted the leader of the troublemakers, the squirrel who first discovered that the Holiday Train lights could be removed. The Pigeon King landed beside Troublemaker Number One and tried to quickly explain. "You need to come with me. You need to hop back on the train and put all those lights back right now."

Troublemaker Number One just laughed. "Why should I do that? Taking them out was fun. Putting them all back doesn't seem fun at all."

The Pigeon King wanted the mischievous squirrel to see reason. He wanted the squirrel to understand that the lights meant kids, and kids meant food. Enough for everyone. But the Pigeon King didn't have the time. Instead, he pecked the squirrel on the head.

"Ow," said the squirrel. *Peck* went the Pigeon King.

"Oww," said the squirrel.

Peck went the Pigeon King.

"OWWW," said the squirrel.

Peck went the Pigeon King

"OKAY!" said the squirrel.

And Troublemaker Number One headed from the snowbank to the slowly moving train. In his right paw he carried one red light bulb. The Pigeon King knew right away that his plan would never work. The train was starting to roll. One squirrel running back and forth with one light bulb at a time would never be able to get all the lights back on the train before it reached the next town.

The Pigeon King needed a new plan. He needed more squirrels. He quickly flew over to the squirrels that he thought of as Troublemakers Two, Three, and Four.

He began to explain. "You need to come with me. You need to hop back on the train." Then he realized he did not have time for an explanation; he needed to skip to the end.

He pecked the closest squirrel on the head.

"Ow," said Troublemaker Number Two.

Peck went the Pigeon King.

"Oww," said Troublemaker Number Three.

Peck went the Pigeon King.

"OWWW," said Troublemaker Number Four.

The Pigeon King leaned back for another round of pecks.

"OKAY!" said Troublemakers Two, Three, and Four. They each ran off to gather light bulbs from the snowbanks.

This plan was better. But it still wasn't enough. He needed more furry-tailed helpers. The Pigeon King flew to the biggest group of laughing squirrels.

He pecked the first squirrel on the head.

"What was that for?" said the squirrel.

"Oh right, sorry. I forgot to explain the plan first. Sorry. I need you to hop back on the train and put all the lights back on," said the Pigeon King.

"And if we don't?" said the squirrel, rubbing the top of his head.

Peck went the Pigeon King.

"That's what I figured," said the squirrel as he ran toward the snowbanks full of light bulbs, followed by his friends.

Before long, the Pigeon King had all of the mischievous squirrels running back and forth between the pile of lights and the rolling Holiday Train. But he knew they would never make it. The train was going faster and faster, while the squirrels were getting slower and slower. As the train was building up momentum, heading toward the next town, his furry-tailed workers were getting tired from running beside the train tracks while carrying one coloured bulb in their paws. The Pigeon King needed more workers and a faster way to and from the train, and he needed to get more bulbs in fewer trips. The Pigeon King flew away from the moving train and headed for the large building with a good roof and lots of space in the rafters for nests.

When he returned with his flock, they all knew the plan. Find a squirrel, fly them from the snowbanks to the train and back. Make sure each squirrel was carrying as many light bulbs as possible. And if the squirrels had any concerns about the new plan, a small peck on the head should answer any questions.

Before long, the Pigeon King was soaring over the Holiday Train, pigeons and squirrels swooping beneath him. Each pigeon carried a squirrel, each squirrel carried four light bulbs, and the occasional loud "Owww" told the Pigeon King that everyone understood the plan.

When the final light was put in place, the entire train lit up in brilliant colours. The bulbs shined and twinkled on the snow as they rounded the final bend before the station. As the brightly lit locomotive came into view, the crowd cheered and clapped for the Holiday Train, as well as its unseen crew of proud pigeons and sore-headed squirrels.

The Amazing Justin Papano was the first one off the train, expecting to see a dark and empty train station. But when he saw the crowds bathed in the glow of thousands of twinkling lights, he figured it must have been some kind of Christmas miracle. He waved to the crowd, shouting, "Merry Christmas, everyone!" and shot fire from his fingertips. One of his favourite tricks.

The Pigeon King watched as the party flowed out of the train and covered every inch of the station. To his left, kids were dropping cookie crumbs in front of the marching band. To his right, children were spilling popcorn as they watched the clowns. Down in front of him, little boys and girls were fumbling with sweet and sticky roasted marshmallows as they watched the magic act.

And to the Pigeon King, it was just like Christmas morning.

Christmastime in the Neighbourhood

IT STARTED LIKE most every other night. My dad was working. He drove a taxi in the city, which meant that when he wasn't driving, he wasn't getting paid. So, with three kids at home, he was driving almost all the time. On this night he was driving a limo. He'd take a few extra shifts with the limo company whenever the family needed extra money, which was almost all the time. He'd finish his nine-hour day behind the wheel of his black and yellow, then home for dinner, then right back behind the wheel — this time a shiny stretch job with tinted windows and a bar in the back. I'm sure every guy at the company bugged the dispatcher for some extra hours, but the guy who picked the drivers liked my dad. It's probably because of all those bonus hours that Christmas was always a big deal in our house.

I know now that Mom and Dad struggled to get by. I didn't know it at the time. But it only makes sense now.

Dad was a new immigrant; moved here and started working, then a year later he sent a letter to Italy asking a girl from the village to move to America and marry him. She did, they had three kids, and he spent his whole life driving that cab. Mom never worked — it simply wasn't done back then. Nice Italian girls stayed home, had babies, and took care of the house. Nice Italian boys went to work. Dad never even took a vacation. Just worked until he was too sick to work anymore. Then he was gone. To him, that was life. Work every day until there are no more days left.

They were not much different than any other family in our neighbourhood. Every day was a struggle, and just making it to payday was a success. But at Christmas, they always went all out. A big dinner — it was the only time of the year my mom would cook rabbit. Dad would make a big deal every winter when he brought it home from the butcher. He would make my big brother carry it in the door, and when the kids gathered around to watch him unwrap the waxy paper, he'd pick up the head to make the rabbit look around the room. Dad would always pretend the rabbit was talking. Saying something like, "Who's hungry?" Or the rabbit would lean over and whisper, "Your papa asked me to come to dinner. He said Mama was making *coniglio bianco*. I don't know what it is, but it sounds delicious!" Dad would have all three kids squealing with laughter until Mom took the rabbit away from Dad and put it in the roasting pan.

I think about cooking rabbit every now and then, but I can never recall how it tastes. I can remember its voice and the smile on Dad's face as he sat behind it, acting like it was a puppet. I smile thinking about Dad pretending that our dinner was alive and sitting up in the butcher paper. Making it cross its legs and swing its arms around while it talked. Sometimes I get lost thinking about the Christmas rabbit talking in my dad's thick Italian accent.

Christmas dinner always came after the late mass on Christmas Eve. All the cousins, uncles, and aunts would drop by and stay late into the night, eating and drinking and singing carols. For us kids, Christmas morning was the big day. There would be tons of presents for each of us three kids. I remember picking my way to the tree in my pyjamas and slippers, wading through a knee-high pile of torn wrapping paper, actually having to dig through the pile to get to the next present. Most years I can remember what I got for Christmas, at least the big presents, like the year I got my ten-speed. But this particular year, I can't remember a single gift I got. I can only remember him.

It was a simple job. Drive the client from the airport to a dinner party, and then drive them to the hotel after the party. Since Dad was booked to drive one client for the whole night, it meant that this guy was someone important. Dad had picked up plenty of important people. Once he even picked up one of the Chicago Cubs. Dad got to drive Rick Sutcliffe from the airport to Lakeview. He had a nice house not too far from Wrigley, Dad had said. Dad knew my brother and I were Cubs fans, and we asked if he got Rick's autograph. Dad said, "No, I never got a chance, but I'll tell you this. Very nice. Good Italiano boy." I don't know what made Dad think that a baseball player from Missouri named Rick could be Italian, but to him it was important. To my brother and me it was hilarious. Every time Sutcliffe was pitching for the Cubbies, my brother and I added Dad's accent to his name. "Now pitching, number forty, Rick Sut-cliff-a."

Dad had driven famous people around before, but this time was different. Dad said he knew it was different even before he met the guy. The guy seemed to be with some friends at the airport but still needed a ride. When the client spotted Dad's sign with the last name written across it, he waved to my dad, then hugged all the people in the family goodbye. All of them. Dad always laughed when he told the story about the man hugging everyone in the group. The mother, the father, both kids, and then the mother again. She was laughing and crying as she said goodbye. The famous stranger waved goodbye, then zipped right over to my dad. He shook Dad's hand and asked his name.

Dad would have replied, "Billy." Not his real name, of course, but that is all anyone ever called him. He must have thought that Giuseppe didn't sound American enough, or maybe he just liked Billy better. But I never heard anyone ever call my dad Giuseppe. Even my mother never called him Giuseppe. She always called him Papa.

The man insisted on putting his own luggage in the trunk and then climbed into the front with my dad and made himself comfortable in the passenger seat. Dad said the passenger was full of questions. How long had he been driving in the city? Did he like the job? Was he married? How many kids? Where did he live? When did he come to Chicago? Had he ever been back to Italy? Did he still have family there?

I'm sure my dad loved having someone to chat with. He was a natural talker, a real people person, always happy to talk. My dad loved few things more than an attentive audience. Sure, people in taxis liked to talk, but never in the limo. No one talks to the limo driver. I'm sure it was one of the things that he liked least about his job. I'm sure for Dad those were some lonely nights behind the wheel. But not tonight. By the time my dad drove from O'Hare to the swanky neighbourhood of Dearborn Park, those two knew each other better than most people know their next-door neighbours.

Dad was buzzed through the main gate. He signed in at the guardhouse, rolled up to the front door of the mansion, and asked his new best friend what time he should be ready to pick him up and take him to his hotel. But the guy said no. He said Dad was going to be his guest at dinner. Dad gave the guy lots of excuses. His wife had already packed him a supper, he wasn't dressed for dinner, and the homeowner hadn't actually invited him.

But the man insisted. Marianna would understand. He was dressed for dinner; in fact, his jacket and slacks were nicer than the man's cardigan, and even better, Dad's tie was black. Plus, the invite was for the man and his wife, and since his wife was back in Pennsylvania, there was a place for my dad at the table.

Dad never talked much about the dinner. When he told this story, he talked about the size of the mansion. He talked about the army of waiters. One person to bring the food, one to follow with the needed cutlery, another immediately behind with the sauce for the dish, and still another to clear it all away the moment you put your fork down. Then they did it again and again through a dozen courses. But that was usually all he would say about the dinner. I imagine Dad skipped the dinner part of the story because he must have felt so out of place at that table. He must have. At home, he ate over a plastic tablecloth on a plate that didn't match any of the others in the cupboard. It was only when I pressed him once about the house that he did add one detail about a conversation they had. Both the man and my dad were deeply religious. Dad was of course Catholic; his client, I would later learn, was a Presbyterian minister. The two got to talking about the significance of small traditions at Christmastime. Like decorating the home with holly and ivy.

Dad explained that the Christmas cracker is a symbol of the season, as well. Dad loved to tell the story of the Christmas cracker each year at the family table, and he started to tell it to the other guest that night at the mansion. Dad told his client that the cracker was made in London in the 1840s. First made by the Honeycutt Company by a guy named Walter Silvestri, an Italian who had once studied to be in the seminary. Dad explained that the paper crown is inside to remind us of King Jesus, and the original colour of the crown was always purple, the colour that used to be reserved for royalty. The toy inside was to symbolize gold, frankincense, and myrrh, the gifts of the Magi. And originally the toy was meant to be given away before the end of the meal. That little piece of paper has religious significance, too. Today it is usually a joke, but originally it was a handwritten verse from the Bible. Even the shiny paper on the outside is meant to reflect the light of Jesus.

When Dad finished the story of the invention of the Christmas cracker, he looked around the table to see that everyone there had been listening to his story, not just the intended audience sitting beside him. The whole table had stopped to hear what he was saying to the famous man. Dad froze. He said he was sure he was about to be thrown out. Then the lady of the house asked him bluntly, "If all of that is true, what about the popping thing inside?"

We had never asked that. A son thinks every word his father says is true. But adults question other adults all the time. Especially a hostess who has been saddled with an unwanted guest. Even better, an old Italian limo driver who was ruining the dinner party by showing up uninvited and then hogging the attention of the guest of honour.

It was the famous man who answered. "The sound is there to make your heart skip a beat. Sometimes we all need that. We forget the excitement of just being alive. The cracker makes your heart skip a beat so that you remember how important each heartbeat is." Dad only ever told me that story once, but I always think of it whenever I hear that sound. I'm reminded that the next heartbeat is the most important one of my life.

Eventually, the dinner was over and it was time to drive to the hotel. As the two buddies rolled through the streets of Chicago, they talked more and more. The long limo was empty behind the two figures sitting up front. Dad was asked to avoid the highways and stick to the streets that had houses with Christmas lights. The route took them past a name that the passenger recognized. The name of the street we lived on. Dad said yes, the kids would still be up, and no, Marianna wouldn't mind if they dropped in. Mom noticed the limo parking outside and knew something was up. She narrated from between the curtains in the front window. "Your dad is home, and he's brought someone with him."

Dad walked in first and called to all of us, but, of course, Mom was already waiting in the doorway. I was sitting in the chair by the television in the next room when I heard her say it.

"You, you, you're Mister Rogers."

He hugged her and said, "Please, call me Fred. You are Marianna; Billy told me all about you. I hope I'm not intruding."

Mom didn't know what to do, what to say, where to stand, or what to do with her hands. She just paced side to side, fixing her hair and repeating, "You're Mister Rogers."

Dad took his coat and asked Mom to get Mister Rogers something to eat and drink. When she came back, she had a platter with meats and cheeses and sweets. She had also changed her dress and switched her slippers for the pair of shiny black shoes that she usually wore to church. Mister Rogers was sitting on the couch with my dad, across the room from my spot beside the TV. My brother and sister stood in front of them, peppering Mister Rogers with questions. What was his neighbourhood really like? Where did he get all those sweaters? How did the trolley work? Mister Rogers answered every question and complimented my brother or sister before each answer.

"That's a great question, Julia, you are a very observant young lady to ask a question like that. My mother actually makes all my sweaters. She knits each one by hand, and after all these shows, she sure has made a lot of cardigans. But she doesn't like it when I wear one that I've worn before, so she just keeps knitting. What a smart question, Julia."

And to my brother, "You are so very observant, Jonathan. The trolley is run by a young man named Michael Keaton. He uses a radio controller that has a switch for forward and back and a button for the bell. I met him one day after a show, and when he said he wanted to be an actor, I offered him a job on the show, and now he runs the trolley. Michael is a wonderful young man, I'm sure he will be a wonderful actor someday."

I didn't ask any questions. I stayed in my spot. I watched the whole evening from that worn-out La-Z-Boy recliner to the left of the television. It was the same spot I sat in when I watched Mister Rogers on TV, and now I was watching him sitting on my couch. I sat there in my little boy jammies, holding on to my favourite toy, a G.I. Joe action figure. I carried Joe everywhere I went, even started telling people to call me Joe. No one did.

Looking back now, I understand it was just a plastic security blanket. But regardless of why I carried that toy, G.I. Joe was sitting on my lap when I met Mister Rogers. Joe and I watched the whole night unfold without either of us ever saying a word. It was more than just being starstruck. I couldn't get over the idea that Mister Rogers would want to talk to me. I could understand why he was talking to the grown-ups and the big kids; they were important. But I was just me. I can see how silly it was now. I could tell he wanted to say hi to me. He was glancing over at me and smiling. Sort of giving me an unspoken invitation. He didn't push me. He was just letting me know it was okay to talk to him, letting me know that he was going to pay attention whenever I did decide to talk. I never said a word, but I watched it all.

Mom offered him a glass of wine, and he asked for water. He never drank alcohol. He skipped the meat Mom offered him, prosciutto and salami. He was a strict vegetarian. I would learn later that he said that he never wanted to eat anything that used to have a mother. He did really seem to enjoy the dessert, though, a pastry called *bocconotto*. It was filled with almonds and covered with icing sugar. *Bocconotto* was usally reserved for the grown-ups when they came to our house after mass on Christmas Eve. He took one almost every time my mother offered them. I think he had three before the night was done.

After a few rounds of questions, he asked about the piano. Dad explained that Mom and the kids all played and that sometimes Mom gave lessons to kids in the neighbourhood. Mister Rogers asked if he could play before he sat down, and after he did, he never left the piano for the rest of the night. He first played "Three Coins in the Fountain," one of my mother's favourites. Dad laughed when Mister Rogers guessed that Dad was a Sinatra fan and played "Summer Wind." Then, Mister Rogers asked my dad if he knew the words to "Fly Me to the Moon," which resulted in my father standing beside the piano, belting out the tune while doing his best impression of Sinatra's signature swinging finger-snapping. That's when the neighbours started showing up.

Apparently, during each trip to the kitchen, my mother had called another neighbour and told them who was sitting at our piano. Mister Rogers handled each new group of fans the same way he had when he met us five fanatics. He asked each of their names, answered all their questions, and got them to join in the singalong. Because of the ever-growing audience, he played all night and had a strange list of song requests. Everything from "Sweet Caroline" to "Yellow Submarine," and with different portions of the Italian neighbourhood showing up at different times, the poor man must have played "That's Amore" four times.

The kids, and many of the parents, asked to hear the songs from his show. Of course, he knew how to play them all; he had actually written most of the songs himself, including the famous theme song. Everyone sang along with the theme song, all the grown-ups glancing at each other and giggling as they sang "Won't You Be My Neighbor?" It was particularly cute considering most of the people in my parents' house that night didn't even have to cross a street to get there. Our tiny front room was packed with neighbours. Kids sat on the floor behind Mister Rogers as he played songs in between the endless stream of questions. Grown-ups stood shoulder to shoulder in every corner as my dad moved every available chair in the house into that tiny room. He'd offer a kitchen chair to one of the ladies to sit down on and apologize for not having more space and more chairs. As if he should have planned better for when the world's biggest TV star drops by.

It was way past every kid's bedtime when Mister Rogers closed the lid on the piano and declined another *bocconotto*. The neighbours started shaking his hand and hugging him and saying their goodbyes. Many of the kids, and more than a few of the ladies, had tears in their eyes when they said goodbye. Mister Rogers hugged them all, thanked them for joining him, of course remembering each of their names, and asked Dad if he wouldn't mind giving him a ride to the hotel. Mister Rogers asked as if Dad were doing him a favour, not just doing his job. Dad went off to get his coat, Mom was saying goodbye to the neighbours at the door, and my siblings were sent upstairs to bed. It appeared to me that I had been forgotten, again, when I realized it was just Mister Rogers and me. I was terrified. Just a small kid with his television hero. But Mister Rogers made that fear all go away with a smile and a song. He stood at the edge of the room, near the doorway out into the hallway. Then he turned to smile at me. What I would call a soft grin, letting me know that it was going to be okay. Whatever it was that I was worried about. Being shy. Meeting my hero. Anything. It was going to be okay. Mostly, I was afraid that he was going to talk to me. Silly, I know, but that's what I was thinking. He looked from me to my toy soldier and back again. Then I was worried that he would ask me a question, and I wouldn't know what to say. But he didn't speak to me; he sang, instead.

He crossed over to the family piano, sat back down, and opened the key cover. He played and sang very quietly. Just loud enough for me to hear. The people saying goodbye at our front door didn't hear. My brother and sister upstairs in their beds didn't hear. He had a song that he wanted to sing for me, and while he wrote it for every child everywhere, this time he sang it just for me. And for the first time, I understood what he meant when he said, "It's you I like." He meant God. He was trying to give children a message from God. The message is that God loves you, and that love is unconditional. He knew audiences would not listen to a song called "God Loves You." The network would not record a song that tells sinners they are loved. The TV stations would not broadcast a song that says nothing is unforgivable. It's hard for people to accept that God loves them — it's much easier to accept when the man on TV with the kind smile says, "It's you I like."

For a little while, that night made our family famous in the neighbourhood. For a few months, everywhere my parents went they had to tell the story of when Mister Rogers dropped by for a visit. Eventually, Dad got very good at telling the best parts of the story. Years later, whenever he watched Mister Rogers with his grandkids, he would ask my children, "Did I ever tell you about the time Mister Rogers came to my house?" My kids would laugh and say, "Yes, Papa," but he would just keep telling the story as if it were the first time they had watched the show together. When Mister Rogers started to sing on the show, Dad would tell the part of the story when the gentlemen in the cardigan spent the night at the family piano. Dad told that story for years, and it got better each time. By the end, my kids did a pretty good impression of Papa telling the Mister Rogers story.

When Dad got sick, he wasn't in the hospital long. He went very quickly. We were standing in the hall outside of Dad's hospital room when the nurse hurried past. She had a determined look, so we followed her in. She went straight to Dad and said, "Billy, you have a phone call." She helped him sit up and passed him the receiver.

When Dad said, "Oh, hello, Fred," everyone knew instantly who it was and why he had called. Dad didn't talk much. He said that yes, all the family had been in to see him. And no, the pain wasn't that bad. We knew that was a lie, and the man on the phone probably did, too. Mostly, Dad listened; everyone in the room was silent. I thought I heard Mister Rogers praying, or maybe he was reading a poem or something from the Bible. But whatever he said or read, it helped. Dad laid back and smiled, thanked him for calling, and then he closed his eyes.

During the eulogy, there was no need to tell the story again. One of my uncles just mentioned my dad's love for storytelling and smiled at the audience when he mentioned how everyone there had heard the legend of the day Mister Rogers came to visit. My youngest was pretty small when Papa passed; sometimes the two men got mixed up in her little head. Sometimes she would say Papa when she meant Mister Rogers, and sometimes she would say Fred when she meant Papa. But that's okay, it happened to me, too. Both men taught me, both helped me, and I miss them both very much.

The Sweet Things

TECHNICALLY, THE DRINKING of alcohol was forbidden, but the way he saw it, he really didn't have much of a choice. Mr. Bunte was really the only person he could talk to outside of the church. Mr. Bunte was the only other person in town who spoke his native tongue, Swedish. That, and he was the only one in town who would rent him a room, making him Vincent's only friend in the small German town of Isselburg. So, maybe sharing a small drink each night wasn't a terrible idea. Besides, the Bible doesn't exactly forbid drinking, just drunkenness. So, a small glass of homemade schnapps between two friends far from home seemed like a fine idea before bed. Still, it was something that maybe the vicar didn't need to know about.

Mr. Bunte always seemed cheery and happy to share. But this time of year, he had plenty to be happy about. He was the only candymaker in town, with only a few weeks before Christmas. As quickly as he could put new candies in his shop window, the people of the town would empty it for him. Each night Mr. Bunte would work alone in his shop, making amazing creations from fruit, sugar, cocoa, and cream. He would hum old Swedish folk tunes and work meticulously on each treat. One at a time he would prepare each creation. He'd make candied peels, Turkish delight, toffees, and Vincent's favourite all-sugar creation called stained glass. Mr. Bunte would carry the pans from place to place in his little shop, never taking his eyes off the candy. He'd pick up the bubbling copper pot and zip across the small kitchen, stirring as he walked. He'd reach for the exact amount of each ingredient without looking up, then quickly step back to get the copper pot back on the fire. Always knowing that the correct temperature mattered more than anything else. Keep the pot hot for hard candy, medium heat for soft candy, and cool temperatures to make chewy candy. One second on the fire too long or too short and the treat would be ruined. This was made all the more difficult by the fact that he worked over an open fire. Too poor to afford a cast-iron stove, or log burner as it would have been called. The old man had to tend the fire at the same time he tended to the candies. Adding wood and stoking the fire, then adding sugar and stirring his pots. He could never afford to waste a single movement. Some treats could take days or even weeks to make, and ingredients were expensive and hard to come by. So, Mr. Bunte could not afford to make any mistakes, and true to the artist he was, he never did.

Vincent had never tasted any of the candies. Early on he had imagined the confectioner making a mistake and offering him a slightly overcooked toffee. But Vincent quickly realized that was never going to happen. He could not afford to buy one for himself, one mouthful of gingerbread would mean he would have to go without supper for a day, or maybe even two. He would never dream of asking his friend for a piece for free. The cost of getting enough almonds and sugar to make one batch of marzipan was more than a choirmaster at a small church would see all year. So, he just had to be happy imagining what each of the sweetmeats tasted like. Besides, he could smell each one as the confectioner moved from spot to spot in the kitchen. Vincent would sit on a stool by the fire, writing out sheet music for his choir and watch the old man work. And how Vincent loved to watch him work.

To Vincent, each creation was a heavenly work of art, but if he had a favourite, it would have to be the sugar plums. That was when the artist really showed off his skills, and his strength. For this treat, Mr. Bunte had to put aside his thin light copper pots and switch to his thick, heavy cast-iron skillet. The pan had to be held at just the perfect height above the fire — that was the only way to correctly regulate the heat, but it meant the thin-shouldered confectioner needed to hold the heavy black pan straight out over the fire as the sugar melted. When the crystals were just about to turn from solid to liquid, the old man would add a single chunk of walnut and begin to roll it around the large pan as he slowly raised it higher and higher.

As the heavy cast-iron pan moved away from the fire, the sugar cooled, clung to the nut, and started to harden. When all the sugar in the pan was stuck around the treat, Mr. Bunte would place it in a wooden bowl until it was cool and the sugar was solid. He would then repeat this process every night for a week. Each time another layer of sugar would be added, the large pan would be moved toward the ceiling and away from the fire until the small Swede was standing on his tiptoes and balancing the pan on both hands above his head. The treat maker started each night knowing that the entire week's work could be ruined at any second. Too much heat on night three meant that a layer of sweetness would become crunchy and inedible. Moving the pan away from the fire too soon on night five meant that the sugar would not harden and would fall off the sugar plum. It was the best treat that Mr. Bunte had in his shop. It was only made by request, and was only bought by the richest people in town. Vincent had never tried one. He was sure he would never try one. But his senses told him that it was the most delicious thing in the world.

It was the night of the feast of Saint Nicholas when Vincent returned to the shopkeeper's place and collapsed onto his stool by the fire. Mr. Bunte was just finishing a sugar plum and set it down in a wooden bowl to cool beside a tray of chocolate-covered toffees. This sugar plum was just two days away from being finished, the final in a group of five. The local cordwain had ordered the five sugar plums for his family for Christmas. The cordwain was the man who supplied the whole town with leather. Everyone from the saddler to the cobbler depended on him for their livelihood. He was a very wealthy man. Maybe the only person in town who could order that many sugar plums, and the order even included one treat for himself; no one else in town could afford the luxury of ordering themselves such a special treat.

As Vincent warmed his hands, the old man moved over to the cupboard where he kept his homemade hooch. The confectioner had trouble getting the jug from the shelf and struggled to get the cork out of the top. He had been holding his cast-iron skillet for so long that night that his arms could barely move below shoulder height. It seemed to Vincent that he poured a lot more booze into his cup than usual. It may have been because of the defeated look on the younger man's face. It may have been because the older man was having trouble controlling his muscles. The thin old candymaker placed the glass in front of his young tenant and smiled down at him. A smile that said, *Please tell me what's wrong.* So, the choirmaster did.

"It's like herding piglets," the younger man said. "I mean, when they are singing, they are really quite good, but the second they stop it's like I'm dealing with animals. They yammer and shift in their seats and kick the pew in front of them. It seems impossible for them to sit still, even for a second. I have to speak to each boy to get their attention, and by the time I've gotten the last one to stop pulling on the collar of the boy in front of him, the first one is back talking to the kid behind him." Vincent threw his head down into his hands. "Why? Why are they like this? Why are little boys always talking, or fighting, or picking their noses?" Vincent looked up at Mr. Bunte, pleading.

"Why? Why? Why are they so fascinated with what is in their nose?"

Mr. Bunte gave Vincent a smile that said, *I can't answer that question, but I understand.* Vincent leaned back on the stool, running both hands through his hair. "The Vigil of the Nativity is just two weeks away. There is no way I will get them to behave for that! I mean, choir practice is just thirty minutes. The nativity mass will be almost two hours.

"The vicar will be conducting the mass himself," Vincent continued pleading, "and you know what his service is like; he's so old it takes him ten minutes to get out of his chair. They will be climbing the walls before the service even begins!"

Then Vincent, realizing that his situation was worse than he had first imagined, stood up and began to pace around the shop. "He will be able to see them. Everyone will be able to see them!" The young choirmaster was overcome. His eyes began darting around the room as if he were looking for an escape route. "Normally they sit in the balcony where the vicar can't see them, or, at least, where he can ignore them. But on Christmas Eve they will be seated in the chancel, right beside the altar. It will be a disaster." Resigned to his fate, Vincent collapsed into his seat by the fire.

Mr. Bunte looked down at Vincent with a small smile and said, "I think I can help," and he began to put on his heavy riding coat. "Take that pot," the confectioner said, pointing to a deep two-handled copper pot, "fill it with water and put it on the fire till it boils." Then, tying his riding coat closed, he said, "And take that bucket, fill it with snow, and put it on the counter to melt." With that final directive, he headed toward the back door and the barn behind the shop.

"Where are you going?" the young man asked, shocked that his only friend was leaving in his time of need.

"I need to see if the cordwain is still up," said the confectioner as he headed out the door with a smile that said "you can trust me."

When the old man returned, the snow in the bucket was half melted and the copper pot was just starting to boil. Before the choirmaster could begin with his list of questions that had been growing since the old Swede left the shop, Mr. Bunte began his story. "When I was young my father owned a small sweet shop outside of Helsingborg. Around this time of the year, his most popular treat was always polkagris. It's actually quite a simple treat to master, and once you've learned the technique, you can make a large quantity very fast and very cheaply." He gave a reassuring smile to the still frantic-looking choirmaster.

Vincent had enjoyed polkagris many times; there weren't many Swedes around who hadn't. It was sort of a national treat. A bite-sized peppermint sugar stick, soft and chewy. Clear, with a coloured stripe twisted around it, like when the polka dancers spin in a circle. The polka candy usually filled the toes of the stockings of good little Swedish children on Christmas morning. Mr. Bunte moved from the bucket to the copper pot, inspecting how well his instructions had been followed. "When we had family visiting for the holidays, my father would pull out a bag of candy that hadn't been sold. He always told me that it was from a recipe that hadn't turned out right, and that we could have as many as we wanted, but only one piece at a time. As a child I never questioned it; I was just happy for the candy. But when I began to apprentice under my father, I was amazed that someone as skilled as him could make mistakes on a candy that is so simple. It wasn't until I became a father that I learned his secret." The old confectioner dipped a gnarled finger into the boiling water to test the temperature, pulled it out without reacting, and smiled at the choirmaster before continuing. "And now I'm going to teach the secret to you. You are going to serve it to the boys, and we will turn the piglets into lambs."

The process was simple. Boil the sugar, stretch the candy, and the polkagris would be finished. Low heat and a little bit of work, and a large batch could be finished very quickly. "What I learned from my father," the reminiscing candymaker said, "is that if you make the polkagris wrong, you can keep your kids quiet all night long." "When made correctly polkagris is chewy and soft, but as my father taught me, if you stretch the candy over and over again, working it into a hard cube, the polkagris will last all night." Then the old man laughed at the memory. "Or at least long enough for the parents to enjoy their meal."

The candy was perfect for an apprentice who was just starting out. The strong mint flavour would mask any mistakes that came from over- or undercooking and would allow the candymaker to use a cheaper form of sugar. The colour of the polka candy often changed, usually to whatever colour the candymaker happened to have handy. That would help keep the cost of the recipe down. However, the one thing that this recipe requires is a pair of strong hands. A quality that was generally lacking in the choirmaster profession.

"That is where the leather comes in," said the candy-maker. "First you practise and then you can make the real thing." Mr. Bunte dropped a long strap of leather into the boiling water. It was a scrap piece of double split hide that he had bought from the cordwain. It was the kind of piece that would go underneath a saddle, stiff and unyielding, perfect for building the muscles of an apprentice. Mr. Bunte demonstrated. "First you pull the leather out of the water, moving your hands from the centre out to the ends, wringing out all the water as you go. When it gets too hot, drop it back into the pot and cool your hands off in the bucket."

"Then what?" asked the worried apprentice.

"Then do it again" was the reply.

Starting that night, this became the new routine. When choir practice had ended, Vincent went home to the candy shop and transcribed the sheet music needed for the next day. As he did that, Mr. Bunte replaced the sweetmeats that had been sold that day. When the old candymaker was done, he would boil the water for his apprentice and drop in the piece of leather. The supple hands of the choirmaster instantly became red and raw from the boiling water, and he could only hold the leather strap a few seconds before dropping it back into the pot and reaching for the melting snow in the bucket. It seemed to him that the leather only got wetter. When he tried to wring out and stretch the strap, almost no water came out. In the hands of the old candymaker, the leather was dried in a flash, and of course, Mr. Bunte never put his hands in the snow. It did, eventually, get easier, and his teacher would often remind him why they were torturing his delicate hands and frail muscles. "Each time you stretch it, it will last one minute longer. Cook it once, pull it once, and you get delicious polkagris. Cook it many times, pull it lots of times, and you get a stick hard enough to keep the piglets quiet all night." This image made the young choirmaster laugh, to him it felt almost as good as dunking his bright-red hands into the bucket of snow.

As the days passed, the apprentice did improve. He had stopped flinching as he pulled the piece of leather out of the boiling water, and he would swear to the old man that he could feel the leather stretching, even if it didn't look like it. Sometimes, to give the apprentice a break, the two men would head out to search for wild peppermint. If there was time before the sunset, the men would search the shady shores of streams or riverbanks, which often hid some of the green leaves and white flowers. Mr. Bunte showed Vincent how to pick the leaves without damaging them and which plants they should leave alone to grow.

After the feast of St. Thomas, just five days away from Christmas Day, the young choirmaster came home to a delicious surprise. One thin stick of the new hard candy. The elderly candymaker broke the piece in half, and both men were silent as they sampled the treat. To Vincent, it was perfection. Besides being the sweetest thing he had ever tasted, he knew it was going to do the job. The sugar had been worked until it was as hard as a stone, which would eliminate any chance that the Vicar would see the little piggies chewing on the treat like it were some kind of toffee.

Even better, the peppermint flavour filled your mouth, and if you took the candy out, the cool air on your tongue made you want to put it back in. It was perfect. The little piggies would be silent for hours. Vincent felt it was devious to manipulate the children in this way. It was too easy. "The flavour feels so refreshing; it seems to coat the throat and rejuvenate the voice," Vincent said as he placed the candy on a music sheet in front of him. "Like drinking cool water after choir or warm wine after carolling."

The old man poured some of his homemade booze and talked about their need to pick some more peppermint; there would be little time to dry out the leaves before his apprentice would make the big batch for the choir. The old man offered up a toast, raising his glass. Vincent laughed and raised the remainder of his candy instead.

That is when he realized their error. Vincent was frozen on his stool, arm raised in the air, a sticky piece of candy pinched between his fingers and a piece of sheet music glued to the candy.

They were doomed.

Vincent could see how it would all unfold. The choirboys would slobber on the treats until their first song, then each one would place a sticky candy on their music stands. When the song was done, they would find music sheets glued together, followed by sticky hands, stained robes, a distracted parish, an angry vicar, and a young choirmaster fired from his first job and forced to roam the streets penniless until he died. He said none of this. He just stared at the piece of candy fused to the scrap of paper and whispered, "Doomed. I am doomed."

With a sympathetic frown, the old Swede ran his hands through his wisp of white hair and whispered, "Maybe we should go look for that peppermint now." Defeated, the two men walked out together into the cold night. It was a pointless search; with the sun long gone, there was no chance of finding any of the plants. It quickly became too dark to risk walking along the riverbanks, so the men just wandered the streets of the town in silence. There was nothing they could do to change the choirmaster's fate. Sugar was essential, and wet sugar was sticky. There was nothing they could do to change that. They continued to walk late into the night. They found no comfort as they walked. Found no answers. Discovered no solutions. Not even another person to share their problems. The only soul they saw was a poor shepherd who had just gotten home from the fields.

The stout and sturdy shepherd walked to the door of his cabin; his wife was there waiting to welcome him home with a hearty meal and a warm hearth. She led him inside, taking his cloak and his crook. The cloak she carried inside; the shepherd's crook she hung on a peg outside the cabin door. When Vincent saw this, his mouth dropped open and he started to run back to the shop as fast as he could. By the time the old man caught up, the water in the deep copper pot was already boiling.

When the choir arrived for the Vigil of the Nativity, each boy received a large piece of hard candy, clear with a red stripe, shaped like a shepherd's crook and hanging from the ledge at the bottom of his music stand. The night was a huge success. The choir sang like angels, and they were as peaceful as lambs. When it was time for the boys to sing, they each hung their candies back on the bottom of their music stand. No sticky pages. No angry vicar. No homeless choirmaster. Everything was perfect.

The only surprise came after the mass. The candies were large and lasted longer than expected. Most of the boys hadn't finished their treats by the end of the night. After the parish was dismissed, Vincent saw several of the boys sharing their candies. Some tentatively letting little sisters have a small taste or begrudgingly letting big brothers have a big bite. Some even breaking off small samples to share with mothers and fathers. It seemed the entire congregation had seen the boys in the choir enjoying their treats between hymns. And now, as Vincent and Mr. Bunte walked home together, it was all anyone was talking about: what they tasted like, who had made them, and how only the boys in the choir could have one.

In the morning Vincent awoke, and his vision was filled with sugar plums. Two of them, sitting on the up-turned wooden box that served as the poor young man's nightstand. Vincent was overwhelmed; this was a kingly gift. It must have meant that the old man worked late into the night last week, or maybe he was up early each day. Vincent had no idea when the candymaker would have had time to complete just one of these treats, let alone two.

Vincent knew what the confectioner intended. These were meant for sharing.

Mr. Bunte had often mentioned the young milkmaid who lived up the hill at the dairy farm with her family. She was Vincent's age, she had lovely fair skin, and she smiled at Vincent every time they passed each other in town. Mr. Bunte would mention each of these things whenever they saw the young maid. The old Swedish man meant for the treats to bring the young couple together.

It was too much to accept. Vincent would never be able to repay him.

The choirmaster looked around his small bedroom. The bed, the dresser, everything but the clothes belonged to the candymaker. The lantern, the chair, the very room itself all belonged to someone else. The choirmaster had nothing to give to the old man, who had already given him so much. Vincent was consumed with sadness. He would never be able to repay him.

Then it came to him, in an old forgotten poem:

Even After All this time
The Sun never says to the Earth, "You owe me."
The Sun never wonders, "How will you repay me?"
The Sun never asks, "What will you now give me?"
And look What happens With a gift like that, It
   lights the whole sky.

The gift is in the giving. Vincent understood that and knew that his friend did, as well.

Right then, Vincent made a promise to himself. He would accept the precious gifts. Tomorrow, he would walk to the home of the young milkmaid and her family. He would wear his best clothes. He would ask for her at her father's door. He would offer to share the sugar plums, letting her have both if she wanted. Then he would ask her to attend the Feast of Saint John the Apostle with him. And at the feast, he would ask her to dance. He beamed at the idea of her saying yes to talking and sharing and dancing. As he laid there in the borrowed bed, he smiled, thinking he could not be happier.

Later, the milkmaid's father would allow him to speak to her. She would share the sugar plums with him but insist that he have the first bite. She would agree to go to the feast with him, and they would dance. Later they would marry and have a lovely house on the hill. But Vincent would see the fair-skinned milkmaid much sooner than he expected.

As Vincent lay in bed, smiling and thinking of the future, the young girl and her father were walking in the front door of the candy shop. Behind them was the baker and his family, followed by the miller and his sons, then the chandler driving his buggy. Before the end of the day, the whole town had come to the store. Everyone was looking for the candies that they had seen the night before.

Very wisely, Mr. Bunte had spent the entire night making what he called Peppermint Crooks, filling every surface of his shop with the treats as Vincent slept. Despite the lack of sleep, the old man felt fit and invigorated when the customers began to filter in with the glow of the rising winter sun.

But when the dairy farmer and his daughter walked to the counter, that's when Mr. Bunte called to his young apprentice and asked him to tend to the customers. Saying that he was too tired and needed a break. The smiling Swede walked into the back, sat down on Vincent's stool, and poured himself a well-deserved drink.

Never Open a Present on Christmas Eve: A Cautionary Tale

IT IS THE worst tradition that has ever been associated with Christmas. You should *never* open a present on Christmas Eve. Listen to me, don't cry, oh come on now. Don't cry. No, no, you shouldn't open a present on Christmas Eve. Trust me, you don't want to. *Shhhh.* Did Jesus open his presents on Christmas Eve? Of course not. That would be impossible. But that's not even really the point. The point is, my child, that when I was growing up my parents would let me open one gift every Christmas Eve before I went to bed, and it is a tradition that I grew to hate. Now, you are very young. And you may be saying that this tradition seems like a great idea. But you are wrong. I'm sorry. I was young like you once, and I thought the same thing. But I learned the hard way that opening a present on Christmas Eve is a terrible tradition.

My earliest memory is of the car ride when my mom explained how the tradition would work. "You can each pick one present to open when we get home." My older brother and I were sitting in the back seat of the family station wagon, headed home from Christmas Eve mass. I remember watching the thick snowflakes fall into the path of the car's headlights, Mom turned halfway around in her front seat, smiling back at us and using her high-pitched Mom voice that she used whenever she thought something was going to be exciting. "Who knows what's under there. Could be anything. You can each choose one and only one present to open before you go to bed."

Dad chimed in with his additional rules, "But first you have to get your pyjamas on and brush your teeth." Then he quickly added, because it had only just occurred to him, "And this doesn't mean you get to stay up late. You're both still going to bed on time."

I had already made my decision. I knew which present I would choose. I would open a thin rectangular box that had been under the tree since it arrived in the mail two weeks ago. Nothing special about the wrapping, it was the name on the tag that convinced me it simply *had* to be the first present I would open. The tag read "To Jeremy, from Your Great-Aunt Muriel." To my little kid's mind, my great-aunt Muriel was the most fascinating person in our family. She lived in England, which I knew was on the other side of the ocean, and to my logic, if you were going to send something from that far away, you would be sure to send a gift of special magnificence. I was wrong. In England, I knew that they had things that we simply didn't have here. Things like tins, lifts, and lorries. To me, those were all rare unimaginable items from England, and any or all of them could be in that package. I was very wrong.

Even her name convinced me that I was making the right choice. Great-Aunt Muriel. Her very title meant she was better than any of my other aunts. To me that meant the gifts from the Great Aunt would be inherently greater than one from my lesser aunts. I was so wrong. I tore open the present as soon as Mom said we could. After, of course, I had brushed my teeth and put on my pyjamas. Opening the thin box did not fill my heart with joy and happiness, just confusion.

My supposedly great aunt Muriel had sent me a pair of monogrammed hankies. My embroidered initials in the corner of a pristine cut of white cotton cloth. I just stared at it. Sure, my dad carried a hankie in his pocket, but it was never in a pressed square, and it certainly was never this clean. I didn't even really know what it was until my mom leaned over my shoulder and tried to make it sound like a good present. "Oh, she sent you your own hankies! She's very thoughtful. Oh, and they have your initials on them. That's very fancy." Finally giving into the realization that I had been given a lousy present, she tried to help me understand. "When you're older you will really appreciate those." I didn't. This time *she* was wrong. I never grew to appreciate hankies; I use Kleenex. Like a normal person.

That night, I just lay in bed and stared at the box. My older brother was in the bunk bed above me, enjoying the gift he had opened, a reading light and the latest book by Stephen King. I fell asleep trying to make sense of the present I had opened. Who would send monogrammed hankies to a kid? Was it a mistake? Was the gift supposed to be sent to my dad? We did have the same initials; maybe tomorrow morning my dad was going to open some rare toy from the other side of the ocean and then this silly mistake could be corrected. Tomorrow morning he would open a package that was mistakenly labelled with his name to find a lorry or lift or tin or whatever it is that British people are talking about when they say "jumper." Then my dad and I would exchange the mismatched gifts, and order would be restored on Christmas morning. But that never happened. Dad got a calendar from my no-longer-great aunt Muriel, and I was left with a pair of cotton hankies with a *J* and a *D* stitched into them. From that year on, my Christmas Eve presents just got worse. The next year was the year of the fire.

Being another year older and another year wiser, I tried to make sure that my Christmas Eve present was a success. I was very specific with my parents when they asked what I wanted. "I want a Captain Copter flying action figure, and I want to open it on Christmas Eve." Being the clever child that I was, when I went to sit on Santa's knee I made sure to ask for a different gift. "I would like a remote-control car like my friend Darren, so we can race each other. And yes, I have been a very good boy this year." I had practised what I was going to tell Santa so I wouldn't get anything wrong. I knew that Santa's presents didn't arrive until Christmas morning, so I kept my two lists divided to preserve my special Christmas Eve gift. I thought I was so smart.

The plan worked perfectly, until the fire. I knew from the shape and size of the package that the Captain Copter flying action figure arrived under the tree the day before Christmas Eve. So, after church and Dad's mandatory nighttime dressing and cleaning, I made for the gift I had been dreaming about since the first time I saw the commercial during Saturday morning cartoons. "Captain Copter soars to the rescue, yeah. With a quick pull of his action ring, the bravest hero in the skies launches from your hand to zoom through the clouds and save the day."

The two smiling boys in the commercial laughed as the plastic wings on the doll's shoulders popped out and the toy lifted off into the sky. It seemed to rise hundreds of feet into the sky with a simple pull of the string. Then the Captain Copter flying action figure landed gently in an open field as the two laughing boys ran up the grass-covered hill. In our living room, it had a very different flight. I wanted the first flight to be special, so I held tight to the white plastic ring on his back and pulled hard. The smiling, handsome Captain Copter whirled in a few quick circles on his launchpad, then bolted for the ceiling fan. The spinning blades of the toy met the spinning blades of the fan, which immediately doubled the toy's velocity and *drastically* changed its direction. The plastic toy and wooden fan blade made a low *clang* sound as the heroic captain zoomed toward my unsuspecting father's back. He was tending the Christmas Eve fire, another long-standing family tradition that would end that year. As the bright red-and-gold, super-speedy toy hurled at my dad's back, he leaned to his left to retrieve the fireplace grill. Captain

Copter buzzed his shoulder, and Dad fell onto his back, with the grill falling onto his chest and the loose glass doors swinging open and clattering on the ground.

The flying captain did look incredible as he ricocheted around the back of the fireplace. He swooped in just low enough to drag his red cape through the flames, with the synthetic material instantly catching and turning the toy into a spinning fireball. Captain Copter, still with his heroic smile dividing his strong jaw, bounced between the fireplace walls and the burning Yule log. Each time the whirling copter hit the flames the airborne fireball swelled. As the Captain pinballed in the fireplace, more sparks shot out from the log, and more embers left the fireplace to land on the hearth, the carpet, and my dad's bare legs. Acting like an airborne bellows, the spinning wings stoked the fire, and the flames quickly filled the opening and began to reach out and lick the bottom edge of the mantelpiece.

The flames from the red-and-gold plastic were in fact bright green and blue. A sign I now know means that the chemicals in the plastic were extremely flammable and far from healthy, especially when burning. As the good captain slowed down, he descended to the logs and gave one last spin of his wings. There was just enough momentum to push him out of the fireplace and onto the carpet in our living room. Dad was already stamping out the sparks and embers that had made it to the floor when the flying ball of fire and half-melted plastic landed at his feet.

I will never forget the sound of Dad shouting as he stomped on my brand-new Christmas toy, Captain Copter's charred face being repeatedly pounded into the carpet by Dad's blue slipper. The captain's melting face angled his eyes upward like he was trying to read the bottom of Dad's slipper.

But brave until the very end, Captain Copter refused to go down without a fight. Dad stomped and stomped, but Captain Copter kept burning. It looked like Dad was trying to start an invisible motorcycle while screaming for my mom to bring the fire extinguisher. When Dad was done smashing my new toy, all that was left was a charred and shattered corpse that was half melted to the living room carpet. Dad opened the window to let the smoke out, but the smell stayed for weeks, and the carpet eventually had to be replaced. I can still see Captain Copter in his plastic puddle in front of the fireplace. His half-melted eyes looking straight at me, telling me what I had just realized. When it came to Christmas Eve, I was cursed.

There was no fire in the fireplace the next year — that tradition was done for good — but the other tradition would continue. After all, I wasn't the only one who got to open a present. My older brother did, too, and together we formulated the perfect plan. Saturday morning cartoons had convinced us once again of what we should ask our parents for. The toy was called The Lakeside Flying Devils, and the commercial showed two plastic planes soaring and diving in a heated dogfight. One yellow, one red. Instead of shooting each other, the combatants needed to catch a ribbon fluttering from the tail of their opponent's plane. The man with the deep voice in the commercial guaranteed that each pilot would need to use all their skills and daring to outwit the other.

My brother is seven years older than me, and he was much wiser when it came to the manipulation of Mom and Dad. He convinced me to wait until Dad was out of the house and Mom had started into her baking. He explained that we would wait until she started singing along with one of her Linda Rondstadt records, a sign that she was in a good mood, and then we would approach her together. I stood beside my brother while he politely interrupted her and told her that he wanted the The Lakeside Flying Devils and that it would be the perfect present to open on Christmas Eve.

Before she could respond, he explained that he knew it was a very big present for one person, then he nudged me forward and told her how the present would be for both of us. That was my cue, and I handed her the picture of the toy from the Sears catalogue. When she put the folded picture in the pocket of her apron, I knew that it had worked. I was sure that my bad luck with picking Christmas Eve presents was over. My brother had chosen the toy, so surely my unlucky streak would end. Besides, this looked like the ultimate present. Adventure, excitement, and daring all wrapped up in a box labelled "The Lakeside Flying Devils."

That Christmas Eve, on the drive home from church, Mom reminded us that we could each open a present before we went to bed, then added with a giggle and a smile that maybe we could open one present that was for the both of us. My brother gave me a wink and a nod, to let me know the plan had worked and that soon we would be duking it out in an epic battle in the clouds. I was sure I would prove to be the most daring pilot in the world; all I needed was to get home and prove it. After I was ready for bed, of course.

The set-up was agony. My dad and brother put the airfield together while I watched. A plastic dome in the middle with two revolving rings at the top. From each ring was a long metal wire with a small plastic plane at the end. There was no need for my brother and me to talk about how we were going to play. We had spent weeks planning out all the details. Who would be yellow and who would be red. Who would chase and who would get the head start. How many games we would play and how we would count the points. We had decided all these things as we laid in our bunk beds in the weeks leading up to Christmas. No visions of sugar plums, we dreamed each night of dogfights and aerial acrobatics.

Finally, after the cardboard control tower and the paper runway were assembled, we were ready for takeoff. My yellow plane went first; I'd get a one lap lead, then the red baron would try to chase me down. The only control was the throttle. I pressed it down all the way and watched my plastic plane zip in a circle. It soared in a big arch, high over the fake windsock. Then it was my brother's chance. He hit the throttle, all the way to the bottom just like I had, and he was hot on my trail. We had agreed to a race of thirty laps. But it would only take ten. Ten laps of two planes circling the same path. Ten laps of two plastic planes flying at the same height. Following the same route at the same speed. Ten laps with no way to turn or weave or dodge or spin or even do a barrel roll. There were no acrobatics, just two planes flying in a circle, the distance between them never changing. Ten laps later we dropped the controllers and never touched the toy again.

By the next December, I had given up on my hopes for Christmas Eve. We left the church, and I knew I was headed for another disappointment. I even thought about not opening a present that night, but my dad picked one out for me. It was a small square box, and Dad smiled as he said that I might want to open it before bed. When I peeled off the paper, I recognized the toy from commercials. Printed on the box was the same catchy phrase as the song in the commercial. And it's true, it was a "marvellous thing," until you touched it.

Dad took me to the top of the stairs and showed me how to get it started. He easily flipped it to the next stair below and caught it with his other hand before it hit the third stair down. He made it look *so* easy. When he gave it back, he reminded me that I still had to go to bed on time, and then he headed off to his La-Z-Boy.

The Slinky bounced down the stairs with ease, and I sat at the top watching it slither from step to step, amazed at how it could crawl, and even more amazed that my hatred for Christmas Eve presents could be so easily wiped away by one silver spring, a marvellous thing.

Then my Slinky hit the landing.

One triangle-shaped stair that turned the staircase to the right toward the living room. They never said in the commercials that the Slinky was unable to turn corners, and it never even tried. It simply slammed itself into the wall and bounced off the landing. Now it was no longer one perfect spring, coiling and uncoiling itself with fluid grace. Now it was two flailing springs with a knot in the middle. Like a wounded octopus, its tentacles flailing about, trying to fight off an invisible attacker.

My dying Slinky continued toward the living room, hitting each wooden stair on the way down. Both halves slamming off each step, only to bounce up in the air, slam off the other arm and form a second tangle, then a third, then a fourth. Until the once perfectly coiled sixty-three feet of tin was a balled-up mass of tangles. By the time it bounced into the living room, there was no way to know where the two ends of the Slinky were. It was rolled up like some sort of 3-D model of a virus. The nucleus, a tight wire ball of silver in the centre, with loopy tentacles stretching out in every direction. Another ruined present.

To my dad's credit, untangling a tangled Slinky is *almost* impossible, but he did it. However, untangling a Slinky without damaging it is impossible. Though he did his best, the Christmas Eve Slinky never did get back to its original shape, and my distaste for this tradition only continued to grow.

There were many more disasters to follow. The next year was the sled; it was the first Christmas in fifty years where we didn't get any snow. The one after that I got a 1,000-piece Supperman puzzle; of course, mine came with only 999. There was the model train set, which didn't come with an engine. Dad told me to use my imagination. Apparently, he got it on sale and couldn't return it.

There was Robbie the Robot, who was supposed to learn thirty-seven different commands, but he never learned a damn thing. You were supposed to say stuff like, "Robbie, speak," or "Robbie, follow me," or "Robbie, dance." He never did any of those things. No matter what I said, Robbie wouldn't listen. When I said, "Robbie, speak," he wouldn't do anything. If I said, "Robbie, follow me," he would zip off in the other direction. "Robbie, dance," and he would spin around for a bit and slam his face into the wall. Sure, I could have pretended that was dancing. But I knew the truth.

There was the year I opened a set of bedsheets. Not Star Wars sheets or Ninja Turtle sheets or cool sheets with footballs or race cars on them, just sheets. Blue cotton sheets. Not even a good thread count.

One year I got the Easy-Bake Oven that I had wanted. Mom read an article that said the toy could start a house fire. She had dad replace the 100-watt bulb with a 40-watt bulb. It never cooked anything.

One year I asked for a Snoopy Sno-cone machine. Some ice got stuck in the grinder. That was the first time I ever got stitches — twelve of them; meanwhile, my big brother was enjoying his new pair of skies.

There was the year Mom and Dad surprised us with a trip to Mexico, and my brother dared me to drink the water. The less said about that present, the better.

Then there was the night I thought I was safe by opening a book. It was a thesaurus. I was disappointed, aghast, crestfallen, and despondent.

There was the year that I got the ice cream maker. That was the year we found out I was lactose intolerant. There was the year I opened the candymaker, which was the year I found out I was diabetic. Then there was the year I got the shaving kit. That was the year I found out I had hemophilia.

The list goes on and on. Every single year. The gift that I get on Christmas Eve is terrible, always. Until now. It is the early hours of December 24th, and you are in my arms. When your mommy told me she was pregnant, I was worried that you would be born today. I was worried you would be born on Christmas Eve, and that because of me, you would be cursed. But I know now that isn't the case. I knew as soon as I held you that you are a blessing. You are wonderful and perfect and your life is going to be filled with love and joy and happiness. The minute your mommy handed you to me, I knew. *I knew.* I knew that you had broken my bad luck streak. I knew. I knew that you would change the way that I look at that this day and every day from here on. I knew. I knew that you were the best gift I had ever been given.

The Greatest Christmas Movie of All Time Ever

MY BOSS IS an idiot. You know that. Unless this is the first time you have ever read this particular newspaper, you already know that. Sure, you may not have known it was him who was the idiot; you may have thought it was the reporter or the fact-checker who screwed up. But I can say without a doubt that if you noticed something stupid on a page in this paper in the last two years, it was most likely his fault. He is the managing editor, after all. But I mean the dumb stuff. Like the title of this piece. There is no need for one of the last two words; the title is fine with either *all time* or *ever*. But saying *all time ever* is redundant and stupid.

At first, I thought he was just forgetful. One Monday he fired a guy named Dave, then on Tuesday he told us he was assigning an important new project to Dave, then on Wednesday he complained that he wasn't seeing any progress on the project and suggested he might have to let Dave go. There was a brief time when I thought he was just in over his head. I kind of felt bad for him. One day he was frustrated with the printers, and as I was walking past, he sighed and said, "I didn't take this job so I could be a manager." I paused to look at the sign on his door that says "Managing Editor," wondering what he thought he was supposed to do other than manage.

I used to think it was an act and he was playing some elaborate joke on everyone in the building. Like the day that he stated Justin Bieber was the modern version of JFK. Seriously. He said those words out loud. One guy guided the U.S. through the Cuban Missile Crisis, the other gets paid to mouth the words to his own songs. I find I sleep better at night when I pretend he was kidding.

There was even a briefly held theory that he was a mole from another newspaper sent to spy on our operation and erode our readership with his feigned incompetence. Then I realized that to be involved in corporate espionage, you probably needed to be able to understand how emails work. He seems to think that reply all means that you want to reply to *all* of the message. So, that theory is out, but it is still a distinct possibility that he was sent to our paper to erode our readership with his incompetence.

Most of the time he's harmless. He stays out of the way. He sits in his very large office. He puts *FYI* at the top of long emails and forwards them for no other reason than to show people that he actually did something. He does the modern equivalent of moving papers around his desk. And that's okay. That's what he's good at. It's only when he gets an idea that he becomes a problem. And that is exactly what this article is: his idea.

"Write a short piece on the best Christmas movie of all time ever." That was his great idea. I had the misfortune of walking past his office when he stepped out, ready to inflict his brilliance on the first subordinate who crossed his path. "Two hundred words on the best Christmas movie, for tomorrow" was all the direction he thought I needed. I, however, made the mistake of asking for some clarification. See, I could have just said yes, sir, and written two hundred words about the biggest-grossing films released in December. Or I could have googled someone's top ten list and changed the order, but I wasn't in the mood. So, I asked, "Highest grossing or best critical reception?" He replied that highest grossing didn't mean anything because movies were cheaper when he was a kid; that's why he doesn't look at the box office numbers. I didn't have the strength to explain what *adjusted for inflation* meant, so I stayed silent. Then he explained that the critics don't know anything about movies. His theory is that they get to see free movies, so they have no idea what the paying customer really wants and that critics see too many movies, so they are too picky about what makes a good film. As he put it, "critics are too critical." Remember I told you he was an idiot.

Using his reasoning, the Christmas 2000 box-office smash, *How the Grinch Stole Christmas*, is out. It made $260 million at the box office, but he doesn't want it on the list because people had to pay twelve bucks to get in. Also, Frank Capra's *It's a Wonderful Life* is out. Critically, it was the highest-rated Christmas movie, but it doesn't make the list because the reviewers got their tickets for free. Plus, *It's a Wonderful Life* was a box-office flop. The movie lost half a million dollars, bankrupting the studio, and it became a hit on television only after the copyright expired in 1974 and networks found out they could show the movie for free. So, the movie that millions of people have watched and loved for decades doesn't make the list.

I told him I'd go with *National Lampoon's Christmas Vacation*. It's only twelfth on the list of highest-grossing holiday films, and most critics didn't like it. He says no. It's got to be something that is really about Christmas and the true spirit of the season. I offer up *The Nativity Story*, which came out in 2006 and did moderately well with audiences and critics, but he hates it. "Nothing too religious," he says. "We don't want to offend anyone by making Christmas all about Jesus." I want to say something about the first six letters of the word *Christmas*, then I realize I would then be forced to watch him spell the word over and over again while he counts on his fingers. Instead, I suggest *A Christmas Carol*, the timeless classic from Charles Dickens where Ebenezer Scrooge learns about charity and the importance of giving, and it all happens on Christmas Eve. I suggest that it is the perfect choice. He asks, "Which one? There are so many versions. You'll never pick one that everyone likes." Okay, he has a point there. The movie has been done to death. The Jim Carrey version did much better at the box office, but the George C. Scott version got much better reviews. There is even a Muppet version, but the less said about that the better. Still, the point of making the list is to share with our readers our informed opinions, not just choose something that no one would disagree with.

His list just keeps getting shorter. *"A Christmas Story,"* I say.

"Nothing where Santa isn't real," he says.

I'm feeling smug, so I respond, "There are no Santa documentaries. In every movie he's a character played by an actor."

He says, "You know what I mean." A light bulb goes off above his head. *"Home Alone.* I loved that one. Write it about *Home Alone.* And include something about the kid who played the kid, whatever happened to him?" Okay, first, *Home Alone* is not a Christmas movie. It's just a movie that happens to occur at Christmas. It could have happened at any other time of the year. There is no "real" Santa Claus, and the moral of the movie is not about the true meaning of Christmas. The message of the movie *Home Alone* is that a few days away from your family is lots of fun, but then after the fourth day, you start to miss them. Anyone who has ever had a long business trip knows that. Plus "the kid who played the kid" is now thirty-two and has a pretty bad drug habit. Not exactly going to fill our readers with the glow of holiday cheer. But I pass on this one by simply pointing out that *Home Alone* is the highest-grossing comedy of all time ever.

I counter with *Die Hard.* He says, "That's not even a Christmas movie." He is wrong. Christmas is integral to the plot of *Die Hard*, and the message from the film is that family being together at Christmas is what matters. Even if you've got to wipe out an entire squad of elite German terrorists to do it, you make sure you are home for the holidays.

"No, no *Die Hard*," he says as he locks his office door, "and no cartoons, or that stop-motion crap, and nothing where everyone just starts singing all of a sudden." I am about to interrupt and ask if he means a musical, but then he says something that I finally agree with. "Or anything that has Tim Allen in it. Everyone hates Tim Allen, especially in a Christmas movie." Agreed. But at this point, he's not leaving me much. For a moment I think about offering up *Ernest Saves Christmas*, but I'm afraid he will like that idea. He pockets his keys, checks his watch, and waves me toward my desk. "Go with whatever you like. You're the writer, go write." He turns and heads out to his parking spot that is five feet from the back door. I'm suddenly reminded that he puts in the least amount of time, does the least amount of work, makes the most money, and parks closest to the building. If this place were fair, he would at least have to park at the far end of the lot, but no.

He's left me little choice, but he never discredited the movie that I had first thought of when we started the conversation so many painful minutes ago.

The greatest Christmas movie of all time ever has to be *Scrooged*. The 1988 comedy classic is everything a Christmas movie should be. It uses the Dickens tale *A Christmas Carol* as its template, but the film creates a new tale involving Bill Murray as Frank Cross, a TV studio executive who forgets the true meaning of Christmas. With the help of the ghosts of Christmas past, present, and future, Frank realizes what the holiday is really all about. It is a timeless film that is filled with humour, drama, and more than a few scenes to melt your heart. Better than any other film, it explains what this holiday really means. Not how it started or what Christmas used to be about. There are other films to tell those stories. It's not the retelling of the fable of the baby in the manger or a modern take on a Bible story that parallels with what's making headlines this week. There are plenty of those stories out there and more are being made all the time. It's not a kids' Christmas movie where Barbie or Dora helps Santa while showing off the newest accessory that your child needs to get if they want to impress their friends, grow up to be successful, and save toy town. There are way too many of those kinds of films, and other than having Christmas in the title, none of them have anything to do with Christmas.

It's pretty far from a Norman Rockwell dream about simpler times when every mall Santa could be the real deal. There are famous films, and remakes of those famous films, if that's what you want. And it is very far removed from most modern Christmas movies. This one has no talking animals, no CGI special effects, thankfully no Tim Allen, and sadly no Bruce Willis.

It's not a musical. You won't get Dino and Bing standing around a piano, leading a room of highly trained singers in a perfectly produced medley of classic Christmas songs. But *Scrooged* does feature one song. One important and perfect song. The vocals come in late, most of the singers are off key, and there is no choreographed dance routine. It happens just like it would happen in real life, if things like that ever did happen in real life. And they only sing the chorus, 'cause that's the only part people ever remember from a song. The song — "Put a Little Love in Your Heart" — cuts right to the point, and it finishes with Bill Murray begging you to sing along, just like you want to. Only ever repeating the chorus, not only 'cause you know it and it's easy to sing along to. But because it is important.

Best of all, *Scrooged* explains what Christmas is all about. The message is clear, genuine, heartfelt, and seemingly spontaneous. It's not sappy, depressing, or preachy. It perfectly explains what Christmas is really all about — maybe not what it once was but what it is right now.

> It's the one night when we all act a little nicer. We smile a little easier. We share a little more. For a couple of hours out of the whole year, we are the people we always hoped we would be. It's a miracle, it's really sort of a miracle 'cause it happens every Christmas Eve.

And Frank Cross, the guy who at one point in the film wanted to staple antlers onto a mouse's head, is walking toward you, speaking right to you:

> If you believe in this pure thing, the miracle will happen and you'll want it again tomorrow! You won't be one of those bastards who says,

"Christmas is once a year and it's a fraud." It's not! It can happen every day! You've just got to want that feeling! You'll want it every day! It can happen to you!

At one point Frank tells the love of his life just to "brush off" the poor people and the needy. Now he's looking right at you with real tears in his eyes, telling you that charity is its own reward, that it is better to give than receive, and that it is never too late to seek forgiveness. Then he gives you his testimony, hoping you will follow his lead:

> I believe in it now. I believe it's gonna happen to me, now. I'm ready for it! And it's great. It's a good feeling. It's better than I've felt in a long time. I'm ready. Have a Merry Christmas. Everybody.

Then, without even a hint of cliché, Calvin walks in and says, "God bless us, everyone."

Scrooged is the greatest Christmas movie of all time ever.

P.S. I quit.

Humbug (Noun): Hoax; Fraud; Rubbish; Nonsense; Hard-Boiled Candy

IT'S HARD TO know what the "real" story was. It has changed so much over the years, and it was a very long time ago. I'm going to try to stick to what I know, but I'll also include the stuff that my family has assumed and the things that I always guessed at. Most of the story came to me from my aunt Victoria, who was asked about the story's origins every Christmas without fail. I always got the impression that she liked the attention this story gave her. As the oldest living relative, she was the only one who actually lived through the story. Also, as the oldest living relative, this was one of the few times when people actually listened to what she had to say. It is unfortunately very common to only pay real attention to the elderly when we need something from them. But it makes me smile when I think that the old bird might have been embellishing the tale whenever people did want to listen, in order to hold on to their attention a little bit longer.

It was made on the first of December 1942, that part was always consistent, but the planning and preparations likely started long before that. So, sometime before the first of December 1942, my grandfather decided that this year he would do things differently. Aunt Victoria often said that it had been "three years without a real Christmas, and they still didn't have a tree until long after the war was over." So, this year, my grandfather was going to do something very rare, if not unique. He was a fairly wealthy man. Not by today's standards, but by wartime standards he was rich and influential. He was a factory foreman. I know that Grandfather told his kids that the mill only made helmets and shovels for the soldiers. But during the war, there was no way they were that busy with just helmets and shovels.

My aunt Victoria talked about being a little girl and waiting at the window to see her father coming home. She talked about waiting for her father to come home so they could eat supper, and seeing him walking home down the hill with all the other men from the mill. If he had owned a car, it would have been sold or put in storage long ago. Gas, or petrol as he said, would have been rationed for the war effort. Along with everything else.

So, he walked. Every day he shuffled along with the rest of the men from the factory; he in his coat and hat, and the workmen in helmets and work clothes.

I imagine that it was during one of those walks that the idea came to him. I imagine him heading down the hill one night, getting the view of the city, seeing smoke in the distance or a far-off pile of rubble or a new air raid siren that had been built in the neighbourhood. He saw it, whatever it was, and it made him want something that would last. Maybe because he lived in a world with mustard gas, air-raid sirens, and carpet bombings, he wanted something he could hold on to. Maybe he wanted something permanent because the neighbour's home that he passed on the way to work one morning could be rubble the next. Maybe that's why he did it. Maybe that's why he decided to do things differently that Christmas. It did cost him a day's pay, that part of the story has stayed the same. Grandfather had a friend and neighbour named Mr. Clarkson, who everybody called Blackie. Aunt Victoria said that Mr. Clarkson got his nickname because of his jet-black hair and beard, but I suspect there was more to the story. One Christmas my grandmother, a few years back, had said that even though the war was on, you could get anything you wanted from good ol' Blackie. A man named Blackie being connected to the black market seems like a solid guess.

When you remember Grandfather's access at the factory, and a friend who dealt in let us say, questionable goods, some more things about this story start to fall into place. It's basic economics. Grandfather controlled everything that went in and out of the factory. Blackie would have wanted access to all the things that would have been restricted because of the war. Tools, sure, the factory had those. Petrol, the factory had its own motor pool. Paper and soap, both rationed during the war, and the factory would have had lots. Even tea, the factory would have received a large ration for the workers. If you needed it, Blackie could get it, but it probably came out of my grandfather's factory. And it would explain why a factory foreman and a black-market dealer were able to make a record. So, it was probably more about that relationship than the day's pay that got the deal done. My grandfather took his copy of *A Christmas Carol* and went to see his pal Blackie. One hour of recording and four generations later, we still have his gift from Christmas 1942.

It's been played after our family's Christmas dinner every year since. From Worthington to here, through four generations, every year since, without fail. Of course, back then they were called phonographs, and you had to wind up the player to use it. Today, well, just finding record needles is almost impossible. But we still listen to it. We rotate where we celebrate each year; sometimes we spread out on big leather couches and overstuffed pillows at my brother's place. But I prefer the times when I host. Granted, his record player is in better shape, and his house is much bigger, but I really like when we all crowd in front of my fireplace after dinner, parents on couches and recliners, kids sprawled out on the floor. All the kids are old enough now to know to keep quiet when the records are on. Not that you're not allowed to talk, in fact, we talk through most of it. You just have to know when to talk. Everyone knows the story, and many of us recite our favourite parts as the records play. Some parts we even all say together, like the opening. The whole family says the opening line.

> Marley was dead: to begin with. There is no doubt whatever about that. The register of his burial was signed by the clergyman, the clerk, the under-taker, and the chief mourner. Scrooge signed it: and Scrooge's name was good upon 'Change, for anything he chose to put his hand to. Old Marley was as dead as a door-nail.
>
> Mind! I don't mean to say that I know, of my own knowledge, what there is particularly dead about a door-nail. I might have been inclined, myself, to regard a coffin-nail as the deadest piece of ironmongery in the trade. But the wisdom of our ancestors is in the simile; and my unhallowed hands shall not disturb it, or the Country's done for. You will therefore permit me to repeat, em-phatically, that Marley was as dead as a door-nail.

The parts where Scrooge speaks always makes me smile; Grandfather's English accent and the fact that he seems to be trying to give a very dramatic reading give this classic Christmas story a lot more laughs than I think the author, Charles Dickens, ever intended. Usually, Mr. Dickens gets another unintentional laugh when Grandfather gets to the description of Ebenezer. The then fifty-two-year-old steel mill foreman and father of three really starts getting into the reading. You can tell that he had been practising be-fore he started recording, even though my Aunt Victoria maintained that her father never read stories to the kids. That was strictly her mother's job. Not only can you tell the old guy had been practising, but he was also really enjoying himself as he read Dickens's description of the main character.

> Oh! But he was a tight-fisted hand at the grindstone, Scrooge! a squeezing, wrenching, grasping, scraping, clutching, covetous old sinner! Hard and sharp as flint, from which no steel had ever struck out generous fire; secret, and self-contained, and solitary as an oyster. The cold within him froze his old features, nipped his pointed nose, shrivelled his cheek, stiffened his gait; made his eyes red, his thin lips blue; and spoke out shrewdly in his grating voice. A frosty rime was on his head, and on his eyebrows, and his wiry chin. He carried his own low temperature always about with him; he iced his office in the dog-days; and didn't thaw it one degree at Christmas.

For me growing up, this faded old record was how the story was supposed to sound. When I was in grade school, we went on a field trip to see it performed at the theatre. I remember thinking that the guy on the stage was doing the voice wrong. I was looking around, wondering why no one else seemed to notice that this guy's voice didn't sound anything like my grandfather. It was in that darkened theatre that I realized that only my family had heard those records. I was much older than I would like to admit.

Being much older now, I still think Grandfather's voice was perfect for the sound of Scrooge. Deep and smooth, like the soft silt on the bottom of a lake. I like that he didn't try to do different voices for the characters. He was reading the story, not acting out the play. He did, however, seem to relish Ebenezer's dialogue, and of course, the old man from Worthington always seems to play it up every time he gets to read that famous phrase: "Bah! Humbug." My niece Candice was the first of the kids to look up the word *humbug*. I think every kid in our large family has asked what the word means, but she was the first one to copy it out of the dictionary and bring it to Christmas dinner. For some reason I think Grandfather would have really liked the idea of a child in his family, so many miles and so many years away, going to the library to learn more about something he had said.

My favourite part of *A Christmas Carol* is the part when Scrooge says to the ghost of his former partner, Jacob Marley, that he doesn't believe in ghosts. Scrooge refuses to accept what he can see and hear because the senses can be easily tricked. It's the part when Grandfather reads,

> "Because," said Scrooge. A little thing affects them. A slight disorder of the stomach makes them cheats. You may be an undigested bit of beef, a blot of mustard, a crumb of cheese, a fragment of an underdone potato. There's more gravy than of grave about you, whatever you are! Humbug, I tell you; humbug!"

I always loved that "more gravy than of grave" line. I still do. As a kid, I used to think about it whenever I was putting gravy on my mashed potatoes. I would think that if I put a lot on my food, I would get to see some cool ghosts. I used to pour so much on that my family would make sure that I got the gravy after everyone else at Christmas dinner. That's another odd tradition we have developed over the years. Everyone at the table avoids passing me the gravy boat.

Now, by no means is the recording perfect. During the reading, my grandfather sometimes stumbled, paused, made mistakes and then had to go back and start a sentence over again. Remember, he was a factory foreman, and I have no proof that he ever received more than a very basic education. At one point the recording just fades out completely as the ghost of Christmas present takes Ebenezer on a tour of his city. My older brother was the first one in our family to read the book along with the recording in order to fill in the missing portion. It's too bad that it's missing from the recording, because it's an important part, and it's always left out of the movies, too. It's a scene where the ghost introduces Scrooge to a pair of ragged, starving children, and Scrooge asks whose children they are.

> "They are Man's," said the Spirit, looking down upon them. "And they cling to me, appealing from their fathers. This boy is Ignorance. This girl is Want. Beware them both, and all of their degree, but most of all beware this boy, for on his brow I see that written which is Doom, unless

the writing be erased. Deny it!" cried the Spirit, stretching out its hand towards the city. "Slander those who tell it ye! Admit it for your factious purposes, and make it worse! And bide the end!"

I don't think Mr. Dickens would appreciate it being excluded from movies and plays. As my older brother the teacher likes to say after the recording resumes, Dickens was a famous advocate for England's poor, uneducated, and orphaned. It made headlines across England when he toured mines to show children as young as seven were being forced to shovel coal. In fact, my brother, who at this point assumes a posture that I would call his "this is going to be on the test" attitude, usually points out that Dickens was writing a pamphlet calling for organized labour and political reform, and he put that project on hold to write *A Christmas Carol*. Dickens believed that the story was a better way to educate and influence people. It's too bad that that part got left out of Grandfather's recording, because it's so right. If we ignore Ignorance and Want, it will be our doom.

We've got lots of different traditions that have developed to go along with our yearly audience with my grandfather. We always listen to the records after dinner but before we open presents. No one ever listens to it by themselves; it just wouldn't be the same. And the order of the records always gets mixed up. See, the labels on two of the five records are almost completely faded, so figuring out which LP goes second and which one goes last is anybody's guess. When the kids were little, one of them would always ask who was reading the story, which usually led to a hurried and hushed explanation of who Great-Grandfather was and where England was. My younger sister always falls asleep; she says it's because she finds his voice relaxing, but I think it's more to do with her three glasses of wine before dinner. My mother is in charge of the volume because she's losing her hearing but refuses to admit it. My older brother always puts the record on, even at my house. For me it is less about the story and more about how we listen to it each Christmas. Those odd little unplanned traditions are what make it special. The feel of a home filled with love. Having your family near you in the quiet moments of the holiday. The familiar hiss and skip of the needle on the very old album. For me, that is the sound of Christmas.

So, there it is. A Christmas tradition passed down since 1942. I think it was a gift from a man living through a difficult time, trying to make something good last. Preserving something to bring his family together, even if they are together for just long enough to hear a story. And it's a good story; it's a story about hope, redemption, and the true spirit of the season. And most importantly, regardless of the reason, we are family and we are together.

So, here I am. No recording studio, just my home computer. Making a recording that will last a lot longer than those five old records ever will. This Christmas it may not be the same when we press play on the remote. But I feel better knowing that this tradition is being kept safe. I think I need that right now. I live in a world where my TV shows nothing but riots and war and violence, while at the same time reminds me that everything I'm seeing is happening now. I think I need a reminder right now that good things last. I want to know that some things never change, and I have to believe that family is forever. So, before I let my grandfather take over, I would like to read the dedication that was given with these records. On December 1, 1942, my grandfather wrote a note to include with the recordings:

> This is my gift for my family, to my wife and children. To those I know and love, and to those I have yet to meet. To those that will someday join us through blessed union and those that will be born and wear our proud name. This gift is for you. May you hear this in a place of comfort, surrounded by love, in times of peace.

> Merry Christmas, and God bless us every one!

Acknowledgements

THIS BOOK WOULD not have been possible without the encouragement, hard work, and dedication of lots of people. Like the author's family. They are a loving and encouraging bunch. But not known for their ability to be quiet for long periods of time. Or any period of time. Which makes it even more special when they gather each Christmas at Grandpa and Grandma's house and do their best to listen intently. Their attention, kindness, and love are always appreciated.

The hard working team at Dundurn Press has been supportive and kind at a time when distance and circumstance made it difficult to do either. Their desire to bring great stories into the world is inspiring. Their support of a first-time author with a desire to tell stories out loud to a very niche audience is extremely courageous. Or foolish. I guess we'll see.

Teachers have played a pivotal role in the writing and the reception of this book. None more than Anne Marie Butters. Her encouragement, patience, and friendship will never be forgotten. She found value in each of these stories and worked hard to help others see it, as well.

Most importantly, the author would not have been able to create these stories without the love, support, and understanding of his wife. She has raised three wonderful children, made several houses into homes, and handled each challenge of their long marriage with dignity and grace. She is beautiful, kind, and writes excellent acknowledgements.

About the Author

JEREMY JOHN IS currently ranked as the sixty-second most famous person from Brantford, Ontario. (Look it up. There are a lot.) His career in broadcasting has included co-hosting shows on 680 NEWS, KiSS FM, and *Breakfast Television*. Jeremy now lives with his wife and kids, plus a dog he pretends not to like, in Sudbury, Ontario.